Five Letters and an Elegy

QUODDAM

DEDICATION

To you Amor, time passes too quickly.

To my parents thank you for my life.

CONTENTS

ACKNOWLEDGMENTS

Thanks to Sandeep for his early comments and encouragement. Doug, for his sharp analysis. I wish I could write as fast as you. Carol for helping me find a copyeditor. Pam for her gimlet eye and exacting corrections. B, for all those long talks deep into morning in the Hailer Ballroom that laid the foundation for this thirty years ago. I'm still waiting for your first novel. Dale, one more foray into the creative world but this time as the manufacturer.

CHAPTER 1

"So Doc, am I Violetta's stand in?"

"Not sure I follow."

"Verdi's opera *La traviata*. Violetta dies of TB. It's all very romantic and sad."

"I see, not really an opera fan. I assure you there is nothing romantic about TB. It kills over a million people world wide every year. Let me be direct, Mr. Altenburg, at this point we have to classify this as XDR-TB, which means the form of tuberculosis you have is resistant to treatment."

"I see."

"It may also be fatal. As a matter of caution, we are going to place you into the HEPA filtered isolation room. We are going to start a new five-drug treatment regimen. It's been shown to be 48 percent effective. We also don't understand how someone as healthy as you developed TB disease. It's unusual. We are still trying to determine the trigger. In many cases of TB disease there is an insult to the immune system, such as HIV. We would like to continue to run tests with your consent. Do you have any questions?"

"You can run all the tests you want. This regime has a 52 percent failure rate to turn the numbers around. Also, am I completely isolated from the outside world? Am I allowed visitors?"

"Well, to address your initial comment about the treatment, yes there is more of a chance you would die but your immune system does not appear to be compromised, so I am optimistic it will work. Also, we don't have stats for effectiveness in the United States since it is extremely rare here. Regarding visitors, there are standard precautions that will need to be taken by you and any visitors – wearing masks, and hand hygiene. We can give you the protocol. Until we get you moved, it would be better not to have any visitors."

"Will you explain this to my brother Conor?"

"Yes, as soon as we are finished here."

"Okay. Thanks doc."

An hour later, a nurse came with a wheelchair to move him. She gave him a mask to wear and within ten minutes he was in a negative pressure and HEPA filtered isolation room. He turned on the TV to occupy his mind while he waited for his personal effects to be brought. He started coughing and it went on until he began to feel desperate to breath. He got out of bed and went into the bathroom. He was steadily losing weight. He understood why it had been given the name consumption. He asked himself, "Am I ready to die?"

The answer he arrived at after a long period of thinking, was that he would not fight it. Either the medicine worked or didn't. Death was equal to living. Inside his head, the voice rattled on: *What has been accomplished in your life? If you die was there any point to your life at all? You kept drifting and never really lived. You filled your days with nothing. Think of the women you loved or who loved you. Where are they today? You have nothing.*

On it went until he could take it no longer. He left the bathroom and went to his window. At least in his new room, he could see out across the parking lot and the surrounding area instead of an exterior wall. A light snow was falling and he watched it blow in the wind under the parking lot lamps. Somewhere in the back of his mind, he heard the voice of his mother talking on the phone, "There is someone for everyone."

Then he looked up and there was an orderly at the door with a cart. She was bringing him his personal effects. He put his mask on before she entered the room. He put everything on his bed and thanked her. He picked up his laptop, sat on his bed, opened it up and began to search for a quote he had once heard in high school Latin. It was 5:00 PM. An hour later, when they brought him his food, he stopped and ate a small amount.

He had to get it out of his head – the thoughts and feelings that had tortured him for years. If he was going to die, then at least he would write out what he felt. He no longer cared if anyone thought him weak. There was an inescapable element of self-pity and the all too human desire to avoid legitimate suffering that drove him, but he was determined to write it down.

Every time the nurses stopped in that evening on their rounds, he was hovering over his keyboard, agonizing over what to type. He had the feelings, the thoughts and he wanted to write while he still could. Despite them telling him he needed his rest he continued to work. *What does it matter?* He thought. *They never let you rest in the hospital. It's a small miracle anyone ever recovers.*

At 4:30 AM he found himself nodding over his laptop and he finally went to sleep. Two hours later they woke him to start his new medicine, then he went back to sleep. Shortly after noon they woke him again to take more medicine. He opened his laptop and began to type. It took two days of constant re-writing before he was satisfied with what he had written.

Five Letters and an Elegy

All he had was a general idea and an introduction, but it was a start. It was how he felt in way he had never expressed to anyone. After he had buried his parents at the age of seventeen, he decided it was futile to share what he felt. He thought to be sad, to grow depressed was weakness and it was worse to share these feelings with others.

CHAPTER 2

It was late in the evening. His brother Conor was speaking with his wife Lettie, having waited until their children were finally in bed. "I need to call Declan and Aidan. The doctor didn't sound very optimistic."

"Is it really that serious? He tends to exaggerate," said Lettie, thinking about her grocery list.

"Are you listening? The doctor is the one who said it is one of the hard to treat strains. He called X, X or something TB. Man, I am getting old I can't remember exactly what he called it. Regardless, he has been in the hospital for nine months. Doesn't that sound serious to you?"

"Oh," his wife said, looking up.

"They are starting this new cocktail of drugs to halt it. If it works he will need to be treated for a year or longer to make sure it's taken care of. If it doesn't work, at this point, he will go pretty quickly — as in over the next two months. He could be dead by March."

"Didn't your brother have a trust like you?"

"What? Oh, yeah, Mom and Dad left one for all four of us. I wonder if there is anything left? He stayed in school forever, traveled around. Plus he doesn't have health insurance."

"Well, God forbid the treatment doesn't work but I was thinking, well... perhaps he could leave it to CJ and Em."

"Really, Lettie? Sometimes you are incredibly crass."

"Someone has to look out for children's best interests."

"Next time I visit, which I don't want to do — God knows how contagious that stuff is. I suppose I can bring it up."

"It only makes sense. Aidan and Sarah don't have children and Declan and Shannon are both doctors. They certainly don't need the money."

"Well, it may make sense, but if you recall, Ryan and I never got along... probably because I had no sympathy for his self-indulgent BS.... And he always admired Declan so he could very easily will it to them even when they don't really need it. So it's going to be delicate. I need to think about how I can approach the subject without being insensitive."

"You're a great attorney, baby. I am sure you will think of something."

"Thanks"

"I will call Declan and Aidan first thing tomorrow. I'm tired. I'm going to bed."

§

The next morning after breakfast, Conor called his office. "Jane, is that you?"

"Yes."

"Where's the receptionist? Oh never mind, I won't be in until around ten this morning. I have some personal business to take care of. Please set my phone to DND so everything goes to voice mail."

"You realize you can set that yourself remotely?"

"Well, yes I know, but it takes, like, ten steps on the keypad and all you have to do is walk in my office and push a button on the phone."

"Right," she said, "talk to you later."

He picked up his cell phone and scrolled through the address book and found his brother Aidan's home number. He found himself muttering out loud, "It's early in Colorado; he will still be at home."

He dialed the number and listened to the ring, impatiently tapping the kitchen table. He heard a woman's voice on the other end. It was Sarah, Aidan's wife.

"Sarah?"

"This is she."

"Hey, it's Conor."

"Oh, hi."

"Is Aidan awake and moving."

"He's still in the shower. You want him to call you back?"

"Please, as soon as he can."

"Is everything okay?"

"Well, it's Ryan. The doctors say he has X, XB, er, XDR-TB. It's rare and technically untreatable but the critical care specialist thinks this new cocktail of drugs offers some hope."

"I'm sorry to hear that. I will have him call as soon as he is out."

"Thanks, talk to you."

"Bye."

"Bye."

He picked up the phone and started to dial Declan. Then he stopped himself and put the phone down. He really didn't feel like calling Declan. He resented his oldest brother. He felt that everything came too easy to him, whereas he had to work tirelessly for everything he had. If he resented Declan, he despised his little brother whom he thought was mentally weak and a dilettante. By his way of thinking his TB was something he brought on himself. He wondered why he had come back to Saint Louis instead of heading to Baltimore where Declan lived. He was stuck coordinating everything. Lettie was less interested in his brother's health than the remnants of his trust. Even for Conor that was callous. His cell phone started to buzz.

"Hello, Conor Altenburg."

"It's me, Conor. What's going on with Ryan?"

"Hey Aidan. Well, it's not good. He has extreme drug resistant tuberculosis. They are basically experimenting on him at this point. You might want to come into town in the next couple weeks. If he doesn't respond to the new treatment, he is going to die."

"Wow…okay. Didn't they just think this was some atypical case of TB disease?"

"Yeah, at first, but he didn't respond to any of the treatments."

"Poor kid. Jeez."

"He's not really a kid, Aidan."

"Yeah, I know. It's just how I think of him. Have you called Declan yet?"

"No, I called you first. You want me to call him?"

"That would be great. I need to get down to the office."

"Conor, look, to get into town I'm going to have clear my calendar. I will be in court this afternoon. I will try to get a continuance on the one next week. If the judge gives it to me, I will fly out next Sunday and be there for a week. "

"You can stay in the guesthouse."

"You sure? I can always get a hotel. Talk to Lettie first."

"I don't need to. Just get in town."

"Okay, thanks. I will call you back this evening to let you know what is going on."

"Very good, talk to you then."

"Okay, bye."

§

Aidan sat down his mind racing with all the things he needed to do before he could leave town. He grabbed his cell phone and said, "Call Declan, office."

The phone dialed and went silent. He heard a voice say, "Altenburg Surgical Associates."

"Hi, this is Aidan Altenburg, Dr. Altenburg's brother. Is he available?"

"He's with a patient Mr. Altenburg. May I take a message?"

"It's kind of important. Could you see if he can spare five minutes?"

"Please hold." He heard classical music. Then, his brother spoke.

"Aidan, it's Declan. What's going on?"

"Ryan has extreme drug resistant TB."

"All right, listen, do me a favor. Find out who his critical care specialist is, would you? I would like to talk to him"

Aidan smiled. Declan was forever giving orders, as though everyone in the world worked for him. "Conor wants us to come into town."

"Right, well, I want to understand where he is in his treatment, what they are doing, what they are not doing and speak to some friends at John Hopkins. I will look at my calendar and make plans to try to be there early next week. Let me call you back in a couple of hours."

"I'll be in court."

"Call me anytime after 6:00 Eastern."

"Okay, that works for me too. Gotta go. Bye."

"Sure, talk to you later."

Aidan clicked *End* on his phone and looked at the time. He needed to get down to the courthouse early to see if he could get a continuance. He called to his wife. "Sarah, are you still here?"

"Yes, I'm in the basement."

His wife came up the stairs and walked into their bedroom.

"I need to fly to Saint Louis on Sunday. It doesn't look good for Ryan."

"Oh Aidan, I'm so sorry."

"Well, what can you do? It's not hopeless but we need to prepare ourselves for him not making it," he said, choking slightly on his words. "I have a ton of stuff to do before I can get out of town."

"Anything I can help you with?"

"Thanks, but unfortunately, no."

"Okay, you let me know if I can help."

She leaned in and kissed him affectionately. "I have to run," she said, betraying a feeling of guilt.

"I know. See you tonight."

§

Declan was trying to listen to the patient explain his discomfort but his mind was on his youngest brother. After their parents had died, he took in his little brother because Aidan was just getting established and Conor was still in law school. He, Declan, was the oldest. It was more of a challenge than he had imagined. He had thought that Ryan was stable since he had been treated for substance abuse the year after his friend moved away. *What was her name?* He couldn't recall it. But he was wrong. Ryan was deeply depressed after the funeral, they all were, but after a month they started to get on with their lives. Unfortunately, Ryan didn't. He refused to return to high school even though Declan and his wife were willing to put him in the best private school in the DC area.

During that period, Ryan made number of fatalistic comments that led Declan to think that he was becoming suicidal. Declan took him out to dinner one evening while his wife searched Ryan's room to make sure he wasn't hiding any alcohol or drugs. She found a slim notebook containing poetry consumed with death and romanticizing suicide, so they had Ryan institutionalized for a month under a doctor's care.

Ryan's first act after his release was to sign up to take the high school equivalency exam. He passed easily and started taking classes at a local two-year college. Everything seemed to go smoothly after that. Later, he transferred to Missouri State because he had some friends from Saint Louis going there. He finished with a major in Philosophy.

After college, Ryan moved to Europe. He stopped contacting Declan and Declan had grown too busy with his surgical practice to really stay in touch. If sisters call weekly, brothers call annually. As Declan sat thinking about his brother, he realized he had only spoken to him three times in the last two years. He felt a pang of guilt because he had spoken more to Aidan and Conor. Maybe it was because they were closer in age and had grown up together. To Declan, it felt like they were two families – one with three children and one with an only child.

CHAPTER 3

Ryan started his letter to Shae. It was hard to not to let bitterness creep into it. He grew increasingly sarcastic throughout the letter, then stopped and deleted the file. He walked up to the window and stared out. It was what he did since moving into the new room whenever he felt frustrated, angry or depressed.

Thinking about Shae, it didn't seem possible that he could have been so easily fooled. In college he would have dumped her early in the relationship. He searched for a reason and then it occurred to him that it was because after Germany he had stopped seeing what was there and started to see what he wanted to be true. He had grown tired of being a user. He was trying to change his behavior but it seemed there was no compromise position. Once he stopped being thoughtlessly selfish and erratic, there was nothing to hold a woman to him. They clung to the uncertainty. It drove them to work for his attention, to give. In a way, he was happy death seemed closer now. He looked at the shadow the hall light threw into his room and tried to convince himself that he did not fear death. A cascade of thoughts washed over him and he continued to stare out the window until it passed.

He returned to his laptop and started to write her again. He typed a single word – *Resignation* – then inserted a page break. This time the words flowed easier, but as he typed, his thoughts grew wilder and wilder. He felt like there was a storm in his mind. He paused to reflect and wondered if he was going crazy – a feeling that never went away from the day that Isabel had left during his childhood. He stopped writing, put his head in his hands, and dozed off for a while. He woke from the stiffness in his neck and started writing again. He wrote, edited and rewrote until late in the afternoon. He looked at what he had written so far - an introduction and one letter. It was a start. He decided that if he was going to die, he would ask his brothers to send the entire document to those women that they could find. What began as a means to empty himself of emotion and frustration might possibly be his last words. He couldn't decide if that mattered or not.

His train of thought was interrupted by a knock at his door. He turned to see his nephew, Josh. He wondered why he was here, since he hadn't seen him in months. Josh had a permanent petulant look upon his face that Ryan detested. He had always found him slightly effeminate because of it, making it hard for him to connect with him. He thought his brother Conor made it worse by bullying him into sports, which Josh hated.

"Uncle Ryan, mind if I come in?"

"Josh, just call me Ryan. How did you get here?"

"Oh, Mom dropped me off."

"I see."

"Yeah, she was taking Emily to volleyball practice and said I should visit you, so here I am. What time is it?"

"It's 3:50. How's school?"

"It sucks. Everyone is lame."

"Yes, well, not much has changed since I was there."

Josh pulled out his phone and started to reply to a text, then began to check his social media sites. A long silence ensued. Ryan sat wondering if his nephew was going to speak anymore. He was so consumed with his phone that he strongly doubted it.

"So Ryan, well…uh…" His voice tailed off as he started to reply to another message.

"Josh, you wanted to say something?"

"Yeah, just a minute," he said, annoyed. "I need to reply to this girl."

"Yes, I see. Messaging your lame friends?"

"Ha, sorta. Oh yeah, do you mind if I take a picture to show my friends? No one has ever seen a picture of someone with TB."

"No pictures. Didn't the nurse tell you?" Ryan said cynically.

"Well, no, " Josh replied, looking puzzled. He could never tell if his uncle was serious or not.

Josh has all the sensitivity of a prison guard, just like his parents. Ryan continued. "Do you know what you want to do for a career?"

"Dude, you asked me that the last time I was here. I want to be journalist, remember?"

"Yes, how could I forget? Journalist, eh? The world needs another sanctimonious fraud. You will be fast friends with economists."

Josh didn't hear him. He was busy texting again.

"What? Economists? Why?"

"They like to tell stories too."

"Okay, yeah, I guess. What time is it?"

"It's three minutes later than the last time you asked."

"I need to get down to the hospital lobby. Mom said she'd pick me up at four," he said. Ryan could tell he was lying. "Gotta run."

He sat for a few minutes more, furiously punching away at his phone's keyboard as if he was trying to dig out a buried coal miner. Then, without another word, he got up and headed toward the exit.

"Enjoyed the visit," Ryan said. "Come back when you can't stay so long."

"Oh right," Josh said over his shoulder. "Funny."

"Man," Josh said out loud as he got onto the elevator, "what was the point in that? That room is like a bad movie and Uncle Ryan is starting to look like a scarecrow."

Ryan smiled to himself. *He'll make a great journalist some day.* He dragged his chair back over to the desk and re-read his letter to Shae. Immediately, his mood soured. Putting in his ear buds, he started to compose the next letter. This one was to Annelie in South Africa. Just thinking of her name made him reach unconsciously for the scar on his cheekbone. He had been thinking for a while about what he wanted to say to her. When he finished, he felt like having a scotch, but there was nothing in his room. The doctors didn't want him drinking.

He walked to the window, looked out briefly, then returned to his letter and added a poem to the end. It was one he had started in South Africa while sitting at the airport, waiting for his flight to leave.

CHAPTER 4

Nighttime came and went and Ryan slept well for a change. He looked at himself in the bathroom mirror but could not tell if he looked worse or better on the new medication. The medical staff came in regularly to feed him his drug cocktail and to take blood. During his last consultation with the critical care specialist, there hadn't been any real progress. The doctor was puzzled, and he adjusted the ratios between the medications, increasing the dosage overall. The doctor wanted him to eat yogurt because of the antibiotics, but it was hard for him to gag down.

He was unable to write, instead thinking only about what he wanted to say. The third letter was to Marie. When he thought of her, anger welled up inside, dissipating into regret. It was his pride and anger that caused him to leave but part of him felt he should have forgiven her and stayed in Germany. He had started out to simply use her for his own pleasure – and fell in love. *Falling in love clouds your judgment making it easier to both say things you regret and withhold things you should say.*

He detested the expression "everything happens for a reason." He once said to a friend, "People love to say it when something bad happens. Sometimes that reason is because you brought it on yourself. Sometimes that reason is because you suck. Sometimes that reason is because you are one of several billion on the planet. It's going to happen to someone. Why not you?"

It was Friday. After he first checked into the hospital, he lost track of which day it was and since had become meticulous about looking at the calendar on his laptop. It had been two weeks since he checked his investments and for a minute he panicked. *Surely, the broker would have called if a trade had gone seriously against me. Worst case, I have enough cash in the bank to cover my medical bills.*

He logged onto his trading platform. He was stunned to find his short position on the South African Rand was up 300 percent. He exited his position. Since his concentration was fading from chronic fatigue, he decided he would be better off going to cash. It would also make it easier to divide up the estate if he died. He started selling every time the market went in his direction. It took the rest of day but he unwound his positions in currencies, futures and stocks. As he looked at his cash balance at the end of the day he wondered if he would ever collect on the loan he had made to Marie's father. He made a note to himself to call his attorney in Germany, who had drawn up the original papers.

He heard a knock at the door and turned to see one of the nurses. She was very attractive but he had no desire left in him. She was a pleasant face and that was all.

"Hi, Ryan. Do you feel like a visitor?"

"Sure, who is it?"

"She said she's your niece."

"Emily?"

"Yes."

Emily walked into the room wearing a mask and washed her hands with the disinfecting foam. Ryan wondered what was going on. First Josh and now Emily. Was Lettie trying to soften him up so he would leave them money? It wouldn't be beneath her. He liked his niece. She was thirteen, with dark red hair and perfect taste in clothes that always made her seem prettier than she was. Her personality was nothing like either Conor or Lettie. In fact, there was something about her calm exterior and warm smile that reminded him of is mother. For that reason, he had a soft spot for her. This was the first time she was visiting by herself.

"Hi, Uncle Ryan. How are you feeling?"

"Tired Em, but that is to be expected. I actually feel a little better today so maybe the new course of drugs is working."

"I hope so," she said and Ryan believed her. Unlike Josh, she wasn't a liar.

"So how's volleyball?"

"Well, we're a new team so we are kind of the best of the worst."

Ryan smiled. "I know what that's like. My first baseball team was the worst of the worst we lost every game but we worked hard and each year we got better and attracted better players."

"We finally got a really good setter. She hasn't played before but she is a fast learner. I wish I had her talent."

"I know what you mean. It's still better to develop a work ethic and tenacity."

"Dad says you never really found a career."

"Oh, is that what he said? I invest. That is what I do. I took the distribution from my trust for five straight years and invested it. And I have grown that significantly. "

"I don't really know what that means but it sounds good," she said smiling.

Ryan laughed and Emily smiled back.

"I have a boyfriend," she unexpectedly blurted out.

That caught Ryan's attention. "Em, you're thirteen, right?"

She nodded.

"That sounds a little young to have a boyfriend."

"How old were you when you had your first girlfriend?"

"Well, same age as you but it didn't turn out well."

"What happened?"

"Her family moved away."

"Were you in love?"

Ryan knew she wasn't really interested in his past. This was about how she felt now. "Why do you ask? Do you think you are in love with this boy?"

"He's the coolest guy I have ever met. He goes to Clayton High School. He's a freshman. We met ice skating at Steinberg Rink."

"What else can you tell me about him?"

"He's a hockey goalie and he wants to study medicine like me. We're in love. I mean it. It's serious."

For a minute, Ryan paused and remembered his time with Isabel. In many respects it was the best summer of his life. He looked at his niece. "Have you spoken to your mom and dad about this?"

"I told Mom. She said it's just puppy love and I'm too young to have a boyfriend. She said there is plenty of time for that."

"It depends Em. Sometimes we know when things are right and sometimes we fool ourselves. At thirteen you can be in love one minute and two weeks from now hate each other."

"Not us. We want to get married after high school and go to the same college."

"Love is not a feeling, Emily. It's not all staring into each others eyes and stealing a kiss when no one is looking." She blushed.

"Love takes commitment. It's doing something nice for someone even when you want to kill him or her. Do you love your brother?"

"Yeah, I guess."

"We love our family but we can't stand to be around them sometimes.

But if they are in trouble, we will drop everything to help them. It's no different with a boyfriend. If you really love him then you won't quit so easily when disagreements happen. And they will happen. The reason young love fails is because we are immature and selfish. Love looks out for the best interest of the other first, not satisfying our own desires."

"He understands me like no one I know," she said.

"Maybe," Ryan replied, "And maybe you are seeing what you want to. It's less important to be understood than to understand."

"It's like he can read my mind. Really, he seems to know what I want before I even say it."

"Emily, listen to yourself. You keep saying me, me, me and me again. What happens the first time you expect him to read your mind and he fails? You will be deeply disappointed. You will question everything about him. I guarantee it."

"Well, it hasn't happened yet."

"How long have you been seeing him?"

"A couple of months."

"That isn't very long in the scheme of things."

"It's long enough that we know we want to be together always."

"I can't tell you if that will happen or not. It's really up to both of you. I do know that it is pretty rare that couples as young as you two are stay together. But if you are really committed to each other —who knows?"

"That's what I tried to tell Mom but she won't listen."

"She is trying to protect you. She only wants what's best for you."

There was a natural pause in the conversation and each thought about what the other had said. Emily thought her uncle was so easy to talk to – unlike her parents. He actually listened and didn't constantly interrupt or grill her like her father.

"Uncle Ryan, I need to leave soon. I have a volleyball game at 6:00. Mom is coming back to pick me up."

"Feel free to leave, Em. I appreciate you stopping by."

"I'll come again. I mean it. Mom told us we had to visit you so you might leave us something in your will. But I don't want anything. I don't want you to give me anything, so you know that when I come to visit it's because I want to, not because I want something."

Ryan's face was expressionless but inside he smiled. He thought of the old cliché, *Out of the mouths of babes.* It would be just a matter of time before Conor or Lettie would show up to try to seal it legally. "I believe you, Emily."

CHAPTER 5

Ryan was reading his letter to Marie, correcting the errors that he found. He had been forced to stop several times from fatigue and it was taking longer to finish each letter. He felt a sense of desperation to finish. Outside, gone was the snow he loved. Two days of rain had brought back the ugliness of winter and he stopped going to the window.

He had two letters left to write: one to a girl whose name he had never learned and Isabel. It was exhausting to bring up the memories. Woman was made for man and man for woman. He never understood what happened. He kept a postcard Isabel had sent him and put it on his little desk in the hospital. He would pick it up occasionally, read the back, and put it down. *What is the point in a single experience?* He wondered. *We have these experiences in life and we think they have meaning or purpose but they don't seem to. You just accumulate scars and perhaps wisdom. You try to pass it on but when it comes to love, we don't listen well. We have to suffer first.* He thought about Emily and wondered how long it would be before she broke up with her boyfriend. *Who was going to be hurt?*

As he started to compose his letter to Isabel, he received a text from his brother Conor that he was going stop by tomorrow morning. *Well, that was even faster than I thought. I suppose he wants to make sure I don't die before he makes his request.*

He thought if he could finish the last two letters and the elegy he could give them to Conor in the morning. Since he was going to give Conor what he wanted, his brother would most likely honor his request to hold on to them until his death. With this goal in mind, he plugged in his ear buds and began to type his letter but he didn't get very far before he became fatigued and had to stop. He climbed into bed just as the chills began. *What is going on? I thought I was getting better.*

Slowly the night dragged on. The fever returned and he began to dream madly. A blur of images passed through his mind. He saw himself at his parents' funeral except he was child. While standing at their grave, two South African policemen came and arrested him. He could see himself laid out on marble slab with coins on his eyes. He watched Isabel enter the room. In his dream she looked nothing like Isabel but he still knew it was she. She removed the coins and kissed his brow. He was struggling to stand but realized he was dead.

The nurse called to him. "Mr. Altenburg are you okay?"

He sat up in bed, soaked in sweat a little embarrassed. "Yes, what happened?"

"You were shouting when I was walking by your room so I came to check on you."

"I was having a stupid nightmare."

"Okay, if you need anything just press the call button."

"What time is it?"

"It's 10:00 AM."

He had only been asleep for an hour. He decided to lie back down and rest some more. *The disease seemed a lot more glamorous when Doc Holliday had it.* He smiled. His mind turned to Isabel and while he was reliving their short time together, he drifted off and slept without interruption for two hours. At noon, the nurse's assistant entered the room with his lunch, waking him up.

"I see you brought me gourmet this time," he said sardonically, reaching for a mask. He could not tell if she was smiling behind her mask. *This one has a stone face.*

"Enjoy," she said and left.

As soon as he started to eat, he was interrupted. "Ryan, I need to take a blood sample." Anton the med tech was one of the few hospital workers who had introduced himself without being asked his name first.

"Of course you do. I think you hang out in the hallway, Anton, waiting for them to deliver food and then you come in."

"Only on Monday, Wednesday and Friday. On the other days I make others miserable. It's in my job description. It says, 'poke with needle before meals to increase nausea.'"

"Success! You deserve a promotion to the proctology lab." Ryan could see that Anton was smiling behind his mask. Anton always seemed to be in a good mood. He held out his arm so that blood could be drawn. He just hoped he could suppress any coughing while the needle was going in. Anton drew two samples this time. He had long since lost track of which days were one and which days were two. The sicker he became, the harder it was to keep track of the routines.

"That's good for now Ryan. I'll be back once you make some more."

"Thanks, that's good to know," Ryan replied and started coughing, bringing up a large amount of sputum into his mouth. He waited for Anton to leave then took one of the bags and spat into it. He was long past the feeling of revulsion. He was reaching the point where he just wanted it over. As he dropped the bag into the biohazard-marked refuse container, the cough returned, this time in spasms of continuous coughs. The pain in his chest was profound.

He kept thinking about his life and despite the treatment, he felt like he was getting worse, weaker. He glanced outside, cursed the rain then pulled his laptop from his desk into his bed and started his letter to Isabel.

One paragraph into the letter and he started to choke. He composed himself and kept typing. To write about the past was to relive it – and he had tried to put it out of his mind long ago.

Surely, I am near death that I have so little control over my emotions that I have grown so maudlin. It was this thought that sharpened his mind. Every word he wrote, he meant. Hours passed and he finished his letter to Isabel, but its completion ruined his mood. He only had the last the letter and the elegy to edit prior to Conor's arrival the next day. It was now early evening and he knew they would be bringing him dinner. Increasingly he had to force himself to eat because he had no appetite. He reminded himself to ask Conor to bring more pajamas. The night sweats caused him to get up in the middle of the night to change.

His favorite nurse, Taylonda, brought in his food for a change instead of an orderly. She was tall and it was obvious that had once been an athlete, though today equally obvious she was a mother. Her eyes were light brown, almost the color of honey and it was in sharp contrast to her dark skin. Once, she sat with him on her day off before they moved him into isolation and they discussed their lives. She had grown up on the near north side of Saint Louis and pulled herself out of poverty through hard work and education. It was her unembarrassed confession of her Christian faith that deeply impressed Ryan. She gave him a New Testament Bible and told him to read the Gospel of John. After his conversion, he could barely remember what his life was like as an atheist. He could recount his father's hatred of religion or his brothers' but he could not recall his own. It was as if that part of his life did not exist.

"Look at you, Ryan Altenburg, lying in that bed feeling sorry for yourself like you're going to die. No woman respects a self-pitying man. I brought you food so you can get back your strength."

"Hi Taylonda, good to see you. What brings you to the pariah floor?"

"My favorite pariah, that's what. A little bird told me you're up here typing away at all hours of the night like a maniac. That tells me you believe this is it and your trying to say it all before you go. I'm here to tell you: don't give up so quickly. You have to fight to live, Ryan."

"Hmm, fight or don't fight, it's not my call."

"It may not be your call but I've seen my share of people who wanted to live and died anyway. I have also seen many more who just gave up and died quickly. Don't be one of those. You're only twenty-eight, barely ten years older than my daughter. You can still have a full life but you have to want it."

"I don't know. It's all the same to me. I find both equal. What's keeping me here? I am not exactly wanted and certainly not needed. My brother Conor sees me as a way to guarantee the financial future of his children. Aidan and Declan have not come once to visit me and I have been here for close to nine months. I understand they may be coming soon. I'm not holding my breath."

"So what? It doesn't matter whether your family loves you or not. That is not the reason for living. There are things you can do. You can love others. And if you had no one on this earth who cared about you, you have the Lord and he will never abandon you. You don't need to be loved to love and serve. It's that simple. Now I have to go back to my floor but I will come back in a couple days and I expect major improvements in your attitude."

"Okay, Taylonda, I will try."

"Don't try, do it. See you soon Ryan."

"Okay, bye."

CHAPTER 6

He was making his final edits to the document. He just needed to give his instructions to Conor and secure his commitment to send it whole if he died. Conor was fussy about being on time so when he said he would stop by at 9:00 AM Sunday, Ryan he knew he would walk through the door exactly at 9:00. In this way, Conor was like their father.

Conor walked in and Ryan put on a mask. He stood to greet his brother and pulled his shoulders back. The tension in the air was immediate and obvious to any outside observer. They were very different people and had they not been brothers, they would have had nothing to talk about.

"Is it safe?" Conor quipped. "Is the Andromeda strain contained?" Conor's insensitivity was on full display. He had no visible concern for his brother's health. Conor was the kind of man who did nice things for people because it made him feel good, not because it was the right thing to do. He came by it honestly; it was part of his personality from childhood. Coupled with a fine mind, it would have made him a good executive in a large corporation. Instead, he had pursued law and then took over his father's practice. His callousness made him a mediocre divorce attorney.

"Come closer brother, my illness blinds me. I want to make sure it's really you." Ryan whispered, knowing his brother's primary concern was his own health.

"Ha, very good. How are you feeling? Because you look like hell."

"I'm dying. What do you tell people?"

"As little as possible."

They both half-smiled like two old enemies sizing the other up in case things escalated into violence. They had had one altercation when Ryan was fifteen. Conor called Ryan out on his reckless behavior and its impact on

20

their mother. Conor was nose to nose with Ryan when a scuffle began, which ended with Ryan choking Conor until he passed out. Ryan apologized afterward, but Conor never forgave him for the blow to his pride.

Ryan gestured to Conor to sit down. "You haven't been by since they moved me into isolation. What brings you here this morning?"

"I wanted to talk to you about estate issues and whether you have taken care of those."

"As matter of fact of I have. My attorney in Springfield is already working on that."

"I see. I was going to say I could handle that for you . . . or Aidan."

"No, it's all being taken care of. Funny thing is both Josh and Emily have stopped by to see me. Em said she didn't want to be in my will."

Conor lost the color in his face. *Lettie, when I get home...* "That's how she is. She isn't materialistic at all."

"It doesn't matter. I have already set up a trust for both of them. I just need one favor from you, Conor."

"You want me to reimburse you for the costs of setting up the trusts?" Conor asked —only because that is what he would have wanted.

"No, that cost is negligible. Regardless of whether I live or not, the trusts are set up for all my nieces and nephews. It's not predicated on my death."

"That's really generous of you Ryan . . . really . . . if I may ask what is the size of the trust?"

"Two million each."

Conor was stunned. He had no idea Ryan had that kind of money. "I'm a little surprised that after paying your hospital bills you have anything left."

"I can trade from anywhere. I only stopped recently. It takes a lot of concentration and focus – more than I can summon now. The currency markets have been good to me. About the favor I need . . ."

"Sure, what is it?"

"I have written some letters to people I was involved with in my past. As it is things didn't work out. You remember Isabel from the old neighborhood?"

"Vaguely."

"Well one of the letters is to her. Take this thumb drive. There are two files on it. One has the information about each person and the last addresses and locations I have for them. The other file contains the five letters with a preface and elegy. I want you to find as many of them as you can and send them a hard copy if I die. I'm sure as a divorce attorney, you know plenty of private detectives who can find people if necessary."

"That's it? That's all you want?"

"Yes."

"No, problem. I would be glad too."

"Thanks, it will mean a lot to me."

"Sure, one thing I forgot to tell you earlier. Aidan will be coming in tomorrow morning and Declan tomorrow evening. They will spend four or five days in Saint Louis before going back."

"I suppose they want to say goodbye – if it comes to that," Ryan said.

"Yes, I suppose. Aidan told me that Declan wants to review your treatment and he has friends that may be able to make some suggestions."

"It doesn't matter," Ryan replied, "It's not important."

"Don't talk like that. You were always such a morose kid."

"No, I wasn't."

"Seriously, ask Declan, you were."

"Well, maybe — I don't remember it that way."

"Try to stay positive. We'll be back on Monday."

Ryan stood up to shake his brother's hand. He was a full two inches taller than Conor and Aidan, but four inches shorter than Declan who, at six feet six, was the tallest of them all. The brothers never hugged after their parents died. When their mother was living she criticized them, along with their father, for not showing any affection.

§

After he left the hospital Conor ran by his office in Clayton to review an agreement. As he was sitting at his computer he remembered the USB drive and opened the file and printed out the whole document. He read the first paragraph of the preface. *Man this is some depressing stuff. I always knew he was full of self-pity, but this is worse than I imagined.*

CHAPTER 7

Lettie looked up from her book to see her husband and his two brothers walking through the front door. Due to travel delays, Aidan and Declan arrived within thirty minutes of each other. Lettie looked hard at Declan. *That's a man.* She had never told Conor that when they were dating, she had made a pass at Declan over the Christmas holidays, even though he was married. It was so subtle that it flew right past Declan. She was glad he hadn't noticed because she was drunk at the time. She loved Conor in her own way, but felt that he had to be pushed constantly to grow the law firm. He fought her for years about advertising on radio. It also annoyed her that Conor was not as decisive as Declan– a man who knew what he wanted and made decisions. He was his own man, always keeping a polite distance and slow to give an opinion.

She got up off the couch to greet her brothers-in-law. "Welcome, it's good to see you both again. I just wish it were under better circumstances. " She tried to appear sympathetic because that was what was expected of a woman. In her heart she thought Ryan was an arrogant jerk and the one time they visited him on his property south of Springfield, he ignored her the whole time. She liked his girlfriend but thought she was a little wild, possibly slutty. *Oh, I wonder what happened to her?*

"Did you have a nice flight?" she asked them.

"No, flying out of Denver we were delayed multiple times due to the snow. I wasn't sure if we were going to be able to leave," Aidan said.

"No delays here." Declan said.

"Can I get you men something to drink? Beer, wine, whiskey?"

"Tell you what Lettie, I will take them out to the guesthouse where they can put their luggage and take a short break. Then we can open a bottle of wine. I have a good cab I think they'll like."

"Sure," Lettie replied. This was Conor's way of saying he wanted some privacy with his brothers. She knew her husband well.

Conor picked up his brief case, grabbed a bottle of cabernet, three glasses, and an opener, and the three men walked out the back door to the guesthouse. "Does it ever bother you to live in the house we grew up in?" Aidan was asking a question that had long been on his mind.

"No, because even though Mom and Dad are dead, the happiest moments of my life have been right here. The kids know this was their grandparents' house and in a way, they treat it reverently. This is where we celebrated the football state championship."

"I remember. I think you played Left Out in that game, Conor," Aidan said.

"You know I played safety the whole fourth quarter after Tom Baring was hurt."

"Is that what that was? I remember a freshman running around on the field like a mad man with a confused look on his face."

"You guys are full of it. I ended the game with an interception." Conor was getting a little red in the face. His brothers did this to him every time because he got worked up so quickly. Twenty-eight years later and all Conor still talked about was high school sports. He would have been a fixture at the games if his son had any athletic ability.

"It's funny how we all played three sports but all Ryan did was that mixed martial arts thing after he quit baseball," Conor observed.

"He got pretty good at it, if I recall correctly. You discovered that on your own, didn't you Conor?" Declan queried. Conor constantly criticized Ryan and Declan defended him. It created a lot of dissension between the brothers.

"Ha, ha, very funny, Declan. I wasn't even trying."

Conor unlocked the door to the guesthouse and they entered. Lettie had made sure the place was spotless. She hadn't gone to bed until 2:00 AM the night before because she was cleaning it. There hadn't been anyone living there since Ryan, when he first was diagnosed with TB.

They dropped their luggage in their rooms and Conor opened the bottle of wine. "I think you'll like this California cabernet, Aidan," Conor shouted over his shoulder. He carefully poured out three equal amounts of wine into the glasses. Declan was back first and Conor handed him his glass. They stood in silence until Aidan returned, took his glass, then spoke. "Here's hoping Ryan recovers."

Then they all took a long drink. "Let me bring you up to date on him," Conor said.

They walked over to the small living area and sat down. "Okay," said Conor, reaching into his briefcase and pulling out a file, "the doctor tells me that they are trying this five drug cocktail and they are seeing strange results. He starts to improve and then he develops a separate lung infection, so they have to combat that and then put him back on the cocktail. The trouble is, he is not really improving and at the current rate of decline, he could be dead in two weeks or two months. The doctor can't say."

Declan said, "I tried to reach the critical care doctor several times to fax me his records but we weren't able to connect. I did get a meeting set up with all the doctors for Tuesday morning and a list of the five drugs they have him on. I shared those with a friend, an infectious disease specialist who is intimately familiar with XDR-TB. He has been to India several times to meet with doctors over there. He thinks those drugs are Ryan's best chance."

Another short silence followed Declan's statement, then Conor spoke again. "I was in to see him yesterday and he doesn't look very strong. He has lost a lot of weight. . ."

"To be expected," Declan interjected.

"Yes, and truthfully I have never seen him so grim. Now, after reading this," he held up the document, "a short remembrance he calls *Five Letters and Elegy*, I don't think he wants to live. He asked me to send it to all the women his letters are addressed to. I have contacted a private investigator I know who owes me a favor and he is going to get me current addresses for everyone he can. I gave Ryan my word I would do that if he died. "

Aidan reached his hand out. "May I see it?"

"Sure." Conor handed it to him. "Now I know this is going to sound really harsh but I have to say it. That document is nauseatingly full of self-pity, which is kind of what I would expect from him."

Declan sat up in his chair. "I haven't read it, but what do you expect from him, Conor? 'Hurray! I'm headed for the grave, break out the party hats!' Cut him some slack. Really, sometimes you are just an ass."

"Sorry, it's hard for me to accept that from him when he had it better than we did."

"What? You can't possibly be serious. You just accused him of self-pity while shamelessly engaging in your own. I'll say this: you've got balls. We were adults when Mom and Dad died — on our own. He was seventeen. If you recall, that's not exactly the best year of your life anyway. He was a drinking for a whole year when he was thirteen and Mom and Dad didn't even notice until he was arrested on the golf course with a bottle of gin. He may have brought it on himself, but no more than anyone else on this planet."

"Shutup Declan. He doesn't need you to defend him," Conor retorted. "Everything always came easy to you anyway —perfect grades, Division I football, turned down pro football to go to medical school - all without breaking a sweat. Well, guess what? Some of us have had to work hard for what we have. Aidan and I aren't like Ryan who inherited his money early in life or you, who got everything effortlessly."

"Hey, don't drag me into this." Aidan protested. "I have nothing to complain about."

"Aidan, I always warned Mom and Dad they were spoiling Conor," Declan said with a sardonic grin. He knew exactly how to push Conor's buttons. Conor only managed to sputter out a string of invective under his breath. He never confronted Declan directly but made comments under his breath or over his shoulder as he left the room.

A long silence followed until Aidan broke it. "While you two were exchanging pleasantries, I was thumbing through the document. I agree with you, Conor. It doesn't look like he wants to live."

"May I have it, Aidan?" Declan asked.

"Sure."

"Let's talk about tomorrow. What time are we going to go visit Ryan? It's up to you, Conor, because you have to work."

"Sometimes he has a rough night so I thought we could call him in the morning around nine and see if he is up to having visitors. I told them not expect me until after lunch."

"I think that's a good plan. Aidan?"

"Yeah, that's fine by me. The earlier the better."

"Well, it's getting late. I am going back up to the house. I will leave you the bottle. What did you think of the wine, Aidan? I know you have quite the collection."

"It's good. I like it. I think the next time I drink it I will pair it with a beef tenderloin. It has that quality where it's crying to be had with food."

"I thought so too. Good night."

"Good night." Aidan said.

After Conor left, Declan poured himself another glass of wine. He started to pour some into Aidan's glass but Aidan held up his hand. "No, thanks, I'm beat. I'm going to watch the news and go to bed."

"Sure, see you in the morning. Sleep well."

"Thanks, you too."

When Aidan had gone, Declan picked up the document and started to read.

FIVE LETTERS

PREFACE

"The part of life we really live is small." For all the rest of existence is not life, but merely time. Vices beset us and surround us on every side, and they do not permit us to rise anew and lift up our eyes for the discernment of truth, but they keep us down when once they have overwhelmed us and we are chained to lust." - Lucius Annaeus Seneca

I

When I was growing up, I frequently heard adults say there was someone for everybody – but this is not true. There are those who will never know anything more than a chain of broken relationships. There are those whose character in some way lacks an intangible quality, guaranteeing failure. Like a genetic mutation, there is a depredation within. Like a universe whose "fine-tuning" is off by a tiny order of magnitude and will never support life, some will never be loved and some will never be satisfied with the love they receive. They will seek and seek but there is no one living on this earth whose love will save them because they are broken. I know because am I one of them.

I suppose I could say these times are different, that the culture has changed, that it was easier for previous generations – but that is to avoid all responsibility. Is the heart of man or the heart of woman really different today? When I survey the landscape of broken relationships, there is only one person who appears more than once. All of my experiences have taught me that eternal romantic love between a man and woman is more desire than truth. We cannot return to Eden. I went back to where the suffering began; there was a place where once the angel stood and there was the promise. Once everyone seemed to know that, "All perfect things precede all imperfect things." I am not so sure who still does.

We live in desire and ignore reality; we can scarcely bear the one and we cannot let go of the other. We are slaves, bound in chains, servants of our own selfish emotions. Hunger blinds us in our youth, and saddens us near the end. For every person sees a different form of partnership, of undying love, a vision created in their own image, benefiting them, fulfilling their own needs. This is the message of the poets, the writers and the filmmakers, a happy, self-centered delusion, to tease and intoxicate us in our youth and ultimately walk us to the cliff. Our narcissism is insatiable and the devil still whispers in our ear, "You will be like God."

If I am at this moment living without despair, it is only because despair has left me to torture another. Despair comes at night and sits on the edge of my bed, stroking my face and telling me all striving is empty and futile. She leans forward, whispering in my ear that there is nothing life can offer me, and then leaves. Despair would trap us between futility and hope so we no longer really live, so that it is not vice that pulls us down but a self-pitying quiescence. I have let go of both for this world.

I feel old and hungry for rest. My desire has been extinguished as only illness can accomplish. For once in my life the chains of desire are broken, the gate is open, and I walk upon the earth no longer hoping for one more lover. Look at your own life. Would not a disease destroying you in inches be more desirable than yearning, more desirable than the endless hunger? The feeling that comes when you do not want it, that departs when you wish it would stay? The feeling that descends upon you in the scent of an autumn wind or the warmth of a spring sun, the echoes of which you hear in a lover's laugh, or the hand you are desperate to grasp but cannot?

II

There is a voice calling to me and I cannot find the source. Perhaps all along it was simply a cocktail of hormones, some of this, some of that, all out of balance, a simple biological urge to drive the mind – a random, thoughtless, complex molecular machine pushing the desire to bond. There is the part that seeks connection, a union and the part of that seeks after pleasure. The most mysterious thing about any single person must surely be his sexuality. No explaining, no amount of reasoning can capture it, no amount of psychoanalysis can express it; it drives behavior, changes moods, end careers and breaks us. I love sex. I hate it with every fiber of my being. It is a wonderful gift that I made into a curse.

Before the manifestation of manhood had expressed itself fully in my body, I knew sexual pleasure. And once you know the pleasure of sex without understanding, you are changed forever. Your emotions barely catch up. It is like a sadistic doctor wiring your brain simply to satiate the queer predilections of his own mind.

Sex is not a shallow pool in which we splash around in innocent laughter, as some believe. Sex is a river in a canyon that seems quiet when you look from a distance. It is a torrid, spinning current that you cannot imagine when you fall in. It is a lonely exile when you know it too young. You want to stop thinking about it, but it never leaves your mind. It separates you from others who do not know. Terrible knowledge sets you adrift, alone, seeking others. When you find them, you use each other, learn nothing and disappear into the black. And still — if given the chance, I would start again. I cannot help myself. The beauty of love with the oneness of sex no matter how short is an inexplicable joy. Like the dog returning to eat his vomit, I would try again.

III

The world is broken, broken at the fall. I understand that I will not die leaving the world a "better place," because that is not possible. It is a sentiment of the egoist, the desperate grasping for immortality, an empty immortality existing as a remembrance in the collective minds of those you leave behind. In truth, the world will be a better place when it is gone for good - no more sorrow, disappointment, hatred or murder. God can begin again.

If the purpose of love is to cling to each other through the sorrows and joys of life, then the nurses who come to visit me are an embodiment of love. Some have visited me outside their required compensated hours. What could motivate them except true love? So here I am, between bouts of pain, scribbling these words. I am a romantic whose belief in romance is dead, a poor writer who cannot find words, a man who sought eternal love and failed. In pain, I beg for death but not even death will listen to my pleas. For a long time I did not believe in God. And then, unable to make sense of life, living in despair, experiencing evil, I believed there was a God but that He despised me and denied me fulfillment, crippling me at birth with a broken spirit. But now, I know it was the only way I would find Him. Surely, that is the only truly good thing that has ever happened in my life.

In the end, I never belonged here. I was forever an alien wandering the earth, the accidental birth, the deeply flawed, unable to find a home or place of rest. My very life was unplanned. I am the accidental child whose arrival destroyed his parents' retirement planning. It is tempting to wish for the shallow life, dancing and smiling among the glimmering superficialities, greedy for small exercises of power over your fellow man, laughing with your friends who lie and cheat on their spouses, oblivious to the hurt, watching your children grow into adults as nothing more than chattel, an extension of your own vanity. At the end I am like Luther, nothing but a beggar. I hold to the cross.

There have been many women in my life, some whom I have hurt or have forgotten and all before I believed in God. It is a sad fact of a broken world that those we loved without condition we sent away and have forgotten - and those that barely loved us, we could never do enough to please. We never feel so deeply as when we are feeling our own sorrow, and are never so shallow as when we witness the pain of others.

I read that, just once in her life, a woman wants to be the object of unrestrained passion from a man. If this is true, then what follows are my final letters to those who, whether they realized it or not, were.

DISCOVERY

January, Saint Louis

The Nameless Love
It was a whisper. Words you could not understand, words to change your life, your life looking ahead to change, changes inside to alter your mind, the mind-altering step toward manhood. In one minute you are happy, thinking of games, super heroes, fast cars and the next you are on a journey to embrace the emptiness, a blind crusader pursuing despair as if it were glory. With arms open wide, you are waiting on the black, dry wind to slowly erode the last remnants of childhood. In the hollow quiet, when the wind has passed, you recognize you are empty inside, that something is missing. That something fills your mind, and you see the face of a beautiful girl. She, like you, is just a child, playing in the park and chasing after her dog that has broken free. She runs into you. Your eyes lock and she looks down because she cannot hold your gaze. Your childhood is dead. You will never laugh the same way, you will never be happy the same way, you will hold out your cup like a beggar and it will be filled with joy, sorrow, responsibility and worry. In just two years, the anger will come that you cannot explain, desire will seize your mind, and she will return while you sleep, only while you dream. You will never see her, never find her again.

Where are you?

We spent those few minutes chasing your dog, laughing, grasping helplessly for the leash. I kept looking at you, and you me. Did I imagine all this? When I handed you the leash and touched your hand, you weakened for just a moment, a flash of weakness, a willingness to submit. I did not know it then, nor could I express what the feelings meant but it was as close to peace as I have known. It was as close to feeling complete as I have experienced. Your skin was soft and I wanted to touch it again because it did not seem real. In innocence, I gently touched your upper arm and you smiled. We could not stop staring at each other. I remember your mother called you and without a word you started to leave. Looking back and smiling, you ran to your mom, your curls dancing on the wind. I stood there watching you, frozen, hearing your mother lecturing you to not let go of the leash. I watched you go; I watched your mother shut you up in a sepulcher and you disappeared from life.

On the first night after I met you, I lay in bed re-living that moment. The melting of my soul into the pleasant past could not bring back the smell of your hair, the clarity of your smile or the softness of your skin. I had the memory, a remembering cut from physical reality. I was alone; I was to be alone.

Every day I returned to the park after doing my homework, too embarrassed to admit why I went. My excuse was that I wanted to fish the small lake they stocked, so I took the tackle box and ultra-light that my father rarely used. I didn't know how to fish but on occasion there was a man there, Mr. Rosenfelt, a retired attorney in his late eighties, who taught me. We became friends. He was a widower whose children were living all over the United States. We fished together nearly every day from that spring into the fall.

One fall day, I saw the sunlight stream through leaves of the trees and it reminded me of the day and time we met. I half expected to see you and I looked longingly at the field where your dog got free. Other times I caught the glimpse of auburn curls on a girl our age and strained to see if it was you. It never was. We were always a step out of time. To this very day, I find myself looking just to see if it's you. No matter how old I have gotten, I know if I saw you I would recognize you. Would you recognize me? Would you feel the same?

One month passed and the details started fading in my child's mind. I would try to re-capture those feelings, to gather that time into my arms but even the physical feelings were gone. I had only the memory of the feeling, the recall of something beautiful, like soothing words drifting away into unintelligible echo.

Two months passed and I was trapped between worlds. I could no longer return to my childhood. I could not make out the edges of the adult world but I wanted to see it. One day I played with toys, the next I stared at girls. However, more than anything, I wanted to be with you. I wanted to get to know you and spend time with you. I imagined what it must be like to build a life together like my parents did. I just couldn't imagine that it would always be out of reach. I went to bed thinking of you; I went to the park seeking you and I told no one.

A full year passed. When I thought I had finally let go, you visited me in a dream of intoxicating peace and nothing in this life was good enough. I know it wasn't you. It was only the memory of you that visited me. It was the cruel trick of firing neurons, triggered by events, learning, born from sleep and the consolidation of experience. There is no peace in understanding or consolation to be drawn from it. Your feelings don't die when the experience ends. They lie dormant, waiting for the image to appear to torture you. I never thought of you as pure metaphor, the unconscious machination of a child hungry for adulthood. It was not a metaphor that woke me from my sleep, but a beautiful girl from whom I learned, "It is not good for the man to be alone."

How could I let go then when my mind at rest would thrust you back into my awareness, leaving me in a melancholic state? The child cannot make sense of or easily control his emotions. With time comes control, but the hurting never goes away. No man will easily express it.

I am facing the sepulcher now and disappearing as you did from me. My hope and unrelenting desire dies unfulfilled. My entire life was spent trying to find that moment again, that point at childhood's end where there was a glimpse of profound love, the realization that we were not meant to be alone, the pure oneness I saw possible in your eyes. Who were you that woke me from childhood's sleep? I could no longer return to my games and toys after I saw you. The memories of that day still haunt me, from that brief meeting, the profound rush of emotions, the overwhelming feelings, the weeks of wondering why I could think of nothing but you. Why did I not learn your name? Why were you taken from me?

The pain of my illness cannot mask the pain of regret that I never could return to that moment. My sister, my child, one day before the fading away of all desire, I hope you find these words.

January, Saint Louis

Dearest Isabel:

They buried my parents in the spring of my junior year of high school, four years after you left. Why did we do what we did? While they lowered the caskets one by one into the ground, as nature was waking from her sleep, I remembered you and the emotions I carried on the day you left; the feeling that we are always leaving and never arriving. Is it strange that I should remember you when we buried my parents? There is no difference between death and separation. When you never see or hear from a person again, it is death.

Again and again I wondered what I did wrong. I used to think that you never felt safe with me because I was a little younger than you, because you would try to protect me, to nurture and love me. What did I offer you? Remember those stupid letters I sent to which you never replied? I learned to fight in every style available to impress you so that one day you would feel safe with me and we would be together again. My parents were more than happy to indulge me because it kept the unplanned child busy. At first, I lost a lot of fights, but I kept getting better. Like romantic love, though, whether one wins or loses, there is a cost.

So that is why I sent those final letters (no one does this anymore), bragging about my fighting so you would know I could protect you. I am embarrassed today thinking about it, but I was growing up and you never answered me. I could not control my passion for you and the silence made me desperate - but desperate for the last time. I learned that lesson well, Isa, to hide my feelings - especially from women.

I walked through the home where you once lived after the funeral — again for sale. I stood in the guest room above the pool house where we spoke of childish things and acted like adults. It felt like I was walking through hell. I could find no pleasure in it. I imagined the day bed that was once there and you and me napping on it during the heat of August. Above our heads the clack, clack of a ceiling fan cooling our bodies in the peace and warmth of being together. I do not know why I tortured myself. I thought I left something living there, a part of us. I thought I could bring it back but it is dead and today, I am dying.

I went mad the day you moved back to California as only a child can, unable to control his emotions, unable to give them words, just watching the demons swim through the blood, clawing at the soul, invading the mind. I was empty. The tears clouded my eyes and I could barely see you wave to me, a look of maternal worry seen on your face from the back of the cab. You told me not to cry because boys need to be strong. You cried when you said you were moving, but you told me not to. I understand now; I did not then.

But Isabel, I failed you. I could not hide my tears as your cab disappeared around the corner and I saw you sobbing. I didn't care anymore; I lost you; the only love I felt in my life. You were a sister, a friend, my first true love. We did things no one so young should because we lived without guidance or supervision. We were raising ourselves; and you, though four months older, seemed so wise.

The day you arrived in the neighborhood was the change I needed. Oppressed with ennui early in my break from school, it promised to be a summer of misery for a boy mostly left to his own devices. My parents always busy with social and charitable commitments, and with no neighborhood children, boredom was the break from school. Despondence was the toy I played with, the one no one wanted, that no thief would steal from your yard. I know you felt the same. Three homes in five years, you told me. The most important thing in the world was your father's career and your mother's charities. We were the outcasts - the afterthoughts who found solace in play and conversation.

I watched with curiosity as you moved in. Your wild blonde hair seemed out of place with your olive skin but it was a striking contrast and I could not stop staring. You looked up the street and smiled at me in your gregarious way and I gave you a feeble wave, and went back inside.

I remember the day my mother told me to go down the street and introduce myself to you since we would share a ride to school in the fall. When you are the first child, your mother drives you to school and weeps afterwards. When you are the unplanned child, she kisses you as you climb out of the back of the vehicle and makes the same face she gives the dog when the ball rolls under the couch. More than anything, what drew me to you was your natural affection for people. On that first drive to school, you prattled on about California and how you couldn't wait to go back while I sat in silence, amazed at the smile radiating from your eyes, how everyone pronounced your name here in English but it was the Spanish spelling and should be pronounced that way. I sat and listened. There was an entire world there and I wanted to belong.

I was the first to be dropped off on the boy's side of the school and before I left, you ran your hand over my buzz cut in unconscious curiosity. I doubt you even remember. The softness of your touch embarrassed me, but in my fascination, I did not resist. I looked you in the eye just longer than was comfortable and got out. Your mother glared at you in the rear view mirror like you had crossed a line. I didn't think so, because even then I knew we were connected.

I began to look forward to the ride to and from school. I couldn't wait for the day to end. We would sit in the back and I would listen to you talk about this girl or this boy, who was dating whom, the current music, fashion, or how I should let my hair grow. Looking back on it, it was such shallow talk but it didn't matter because it was you who spoke. You shared it with me and that made it wonderful. Did you ever feel the same for long? When you arrived back in California, were you still thinking of me?

Remember when you turned thirteen and could sit in the front seat? We didn't talk nearly as much. Sometimes our four-month difference in age felt like ten years. It was as if one grade difference in school was permission to pretend like you were an adult. It was even worse when your girlfriends were around. Sometimes you treated me like a little kid then later apologized when we were alone. I understand now; you were just trying to fit in, to find your own place in a new school. I did not understand then; I just hurt and told myself it wasn't important. And despite these small insults in the beginning, we drew closer and closer. I thought long and hard what it was that brought us together. Why was it so natural that we became close? It is a profound mystery.

Even my brother Conor (I was in his guesthouse until they put me in isolation; he took over Dad's law practice), noticed and teased me. I never mentioned that to you.

"Hey Mom," he shouted one morning after stopping at the house, "I believe the runt has a crush on that girl down the street. I've never seen him get ready on time. She's too pretty for you, runt."

"Leave him alone, Conor," Mom replied.

I was the target of an endless barrage of criticism from him. I think that is why I had no self-confidence when we met. By the time you are twenty-six you can no longer remember what you were like at twelve. You have re-imagined your entire past. You have re-invented yourself. You never read comic books or played dorky games; if you were average in sports, you were good at sports, and if you were good at sports, you could have turned professional if only your dad had pushed you harder. And of course, you always liked girls.

And for me, the latter really was true. I liked girls from the time I was in kindergarten but I could not explain why. Sarah and I would hold hands in kindergarten while walking to lunch. We would sit together until the others began to tease us. These friendships with girls were pure and platonic. It was not like what we had, Isabel. We grew close and we fell in. And everything is different after the fall.

School disappeared into the last stages of spring and your mother took you for four weeks to stay with your grandmother in Miami so your father could focus on work. That was our first good-bye. It was the easy one. After two weeks I grew listless and read everything I could to occupy my time. I walked down to the park and fished with Mr. Rosenfelt but it wasn't the same. He asked about you. He even remembered your name.

"Pretty little thing," he said.

I missed you and I was drifting into the darkness neither for the first nor the last time. Much of my life has been on the edge of the shadow and the light. I guess you really wouldn't know that. One day, when I was particularly down, I got your silly tourist postcard. You wrote,

Miss you,

Isa

And my mood lifted. I still have that postcard. It was the only one I ever kept from anyone. It is the only written evidence that you cared about me. Even as I write this, it sits on my hospital desk. When I got it from you, I kept reading it over and over again, right up until the week before you came back. I wrote you a poem the day before you left Saint Louis but I was too embarrassed to give it to you. It is silly and childish, but I want you to have it.

Come to me night
and rest your hand upon my shoulder.
Come to me night
and lead me to where my love waits.
Chase away the day and thoughts of the day
drive them deep into my imagination.
Come to me night.
My heart yearns for her touch
and my soul her tenderness.
Come quickly night
I love her gentle affection
Come to me night
Soon she is leaving

She is leaving
and I will fade from life.

The day you returned from your grandmother's in Miami, you saw me first, on my way home from the park. You ran up the street, calling to me. You ran like such a girl, such an elegant and feminine girl. I was completely absorbed by your movement and it was then that something shifted; my guard was down and we embraced for a long time. When we let go we looked around but no one noticed. Even at the end, when you left, our parents were purposely blind to what passed between us because they were so preoccupied with their own lives. I remember your first words to me after we hugged. "You have wavy hair. You let it grow. It looks nice."

I shouldn't have cared so much for your small compliment but I did. You smiled at me in the way that pushed back the pressing world and invited me in. The contours of your smiles and the peaceful shores of your eyes are the most precious memories I have. At the end of our embrace, you looked at me differently too. You were evaluating me in a way you had never done before, like we were just getting to know each other. *"...at every meeting we are meeting a stranger."* I was taller than you and I scarcely noticed. We both discovered something unspoken and unexpressed. It remained so among our words and actions until that day.

We built a routine almost like a couple starting a life together. Late morning to the park, to fish where you always refused to take anything you caught off the hook. We went back to our homes for lunch and then we would swim at your house or mine. Late afternoon you would have to practice the piano. Remember the first time I heard you play Beethoven's Sonata No. 14? I made you play it *ad nauseam* after that in truth only to tease you. Now it plays in the background as I write this, a reminder of two months of near perfection that led to the wasteland of my life.

We were rarely together in the evening. I had baseball practice or games and you had dance. I never saw you dance ballet and you never saw me play baseball. Funny, I don't know why.

One day, while you were practicing, your father came home early to pack for a trip to Brazil. Do you recall? He said casually to you in his Cuban accent, *"Mija*, we are going to the symphony next Friday after I get back. Should I get a ticket for Ryan?"

You looked at me with those eyes that shone with pure joy and said, "Yes."

"He should check with his parents first. Next Friday from 8:00 PM to 10:00 PM roughly, let Isabel know tonight if possible so I can hold the tickets at work."

I said, "Yes, sir," and you giggled.

The timer rang and your practice session ended. "Let's go to your house, before you have to go to baseball practice."

"Sure," I replied.

On the way, you turned to me and said, "I am so excited. We never do anything together as a family and you get to be there too."

Then you blushed. I was too blind to consciously understand the meaning, but I felt the same way. I just couldn't say it.

We carried on our unremarkable summer schedule until Friday arrived. I have no recollection all the things we talked about because they have been lost over the years. My journals that my brother Declan found in a box after the funeral tell a slightly different story of my life. The memory of our past changes every time we remember. It was painful and embarrassing to read the thoughts of a thirteen-year-old boy. From those journals, I know we sometimes just sat quietly and read, or we took a walk without speaking – just an occasional glance and your unforgettable smile. It's written there exactly like that. "Isa has an unforgettable smile. She can make any bad day good."

Our friendship was as deep as any two people our age could have. Was that only my perception? Do you think that we would still be close friends if we hadn't become intimate? Everything changed after that. I ached when we were apart and felt like a giant when you came close. No woman can fully understand the power of her affection on a man who loves her -- regardless of age.

Inside one of those journals, I found the program to the Symphony from that night, Polonaise numbers, 2, 6, & 10 by Chopin and Samuel Barber's *Adagio for Strings*, which is forever etched into my mind. It was the arc of our time together - the gentle start, tumultuous separation, and placid acceptance. I cannot bear to listen to it.

I got ready that night and I was suddenly concerned with my appearance. Mom kept reminding me to mind my manners and be polite. I kissed her and walked to your house. Your mom answered the door and let me in; she called you. I saw you come down the long hall where the bedrooms were. You wore a dress. I will never forget. I had never seen you in a dress before and I never wanted to see you in anything else afterwards. Your usual self-confidence was gone. You looked a little shy walking up to me.

"Hi," I said. "You look nice."

You looked more than nice but that is all I could manage to express. My feelings never seem to escape my mouth and I suppose it is my mortality that permits them to escape through my hand.

"Thank you," you replied. "You look nice too."

"Great," your father said, winking at your mom. "Everyone looks nice. Let's go so we are on time."

As we walked out the door, you stopped me and straightened my tie.

"My mom already did that," I said, annoyed.

"Well, it's perfect now," you smiled.

The company your father worked for had incredible seats. I was glad no customer wanted them. You sat between your father and me. You looked so happy, so deeply moved by the music. You have the soul of an artist, Isa. I hope that part of you has not been killed by the sorrow of life.

During intermission your mother asked me a lot of questions about school and my family's summer plans. She reminded me again that she and my mom were both on the board of directors for that charitable foundation, the name of which escapes me. Your father asked me about baseball. Actually, he grilled me. I remember it went something like this:

"You play *béisbol*?"

"Yes, sir."

"What position?"

"First base."

"I can see that you're tall for your age. Where do you bat in the order?"

"Lead off."

"Hmmm, did I tell you I played in college? What's your batting average?"

On it went until they started with chimes reminding everyone to return to their seats. That was the longest conversation I had with your parents. You looked so uncomfortable. On our way back into the concert hall, we ran into two girls from your class. They were staring at me while saying hello to you. Instead of moving away from me like you did when we first rode to school you moved closer to me. At the time, I thought you were getting out of the way of a passing man. Now I know it was possessiveness. I went out with both of those girls after you left. It was as if being with you altered their perception of me. I learned to use that again and again. After you left I just drifted from one girl to the next until I left college.

Back in our seats, the lights dimmed and the conductor

returned to the podium. As the orchestra began to play you relaxed your leg against mine. At the time I thought it was accidental. I felt my pulse quicken to the point I could feel it in my ears. Then, halfway through the first movement, I reached out and took your hand in mine as natural as drawing a breath. We sat there listening with our eyes closed, absorbed in the music. Eden is gone but there are times we travel close -- if only for a brief moment.

As quickly as it began it ended. You father looked over at you when the applause began but I was no longer holding your hand. You looked at me with such joy. We walked back to valet parking with you hanging on to your father's arm. The ride home was quiet and peaceful. I wanted to slide across the seat and sit next you.

We didn't see each other the following week. I went to tennis camp because Mom didn't think I was busy enough. I was angry then; I can smile now. Sometimes in the afternoon coming back from camp I would see preparing for your dance class through the giant picture window. I loved to watch you move even if it was just a few seconds.

I remember I didn't see you again until Monday. I cannot remember why. There was nothing in my journal. What I do remember is I tried to fall back into our routine but you said no.

"I hate fishing," you said.

I was surprised. I had no idea. When we are young we miss all the obvious things.

"What do you want to do?" I asked. You smiled and took my hand. We went through the gate into the pool house up the stairs to the overhead apartment you led me. Inside, you closed the door.

"I want to dance."

I hated dancing. I couldn't do it. You insisted, remember? I kept saying no and I sat down. For the first time, you grew angry with me.

"We always do what you want. When I ask for one small thing, you say no."

I relented because it was true and you taught me how to dance, or at least, how to avoid looking foolish. I learned to like dancing with you. I never thought I would. We would just put on music and dance. I finally understood dancers. At times I completely lost myself. I felt so close to you then. On some days I began to wonder where I ended and you began. This was my unspoken possessive nature.

You asked me to read you poetry on days when it rained. You

loved Verlaine and I read out loud all of *Poèmes saturniens.* You would giggle at my pronunciation but my mom wasn't a French teacher like yours.

During our last three weeks together, dancing replaced fishing and I didn't miss it at all. When I went back to fish on the lake after you left, I found out Mr. Rosenfelt was dead. It was like a kick in the stomach. In some ways, he was more of a father to me than my own father was. I guess it was because he had more time for me.

I still wonder how long you knew that your father was offered the CEO position with that company in San Francisco. In retrospect, it must have been the day before we started dancing. You wanted to do things that made you happy because our time was short.

That day we were in the pool talking and throwing the ball back and forth, your mom came outside and made us get out because she needed to go shopping. She was crabby and annoyed and you argued with her. She threatened to send me home and you inside. I was already out drying off when you finally climbed the ladder. I didn't understand the conflict.

When your mom was gone you walked into the pool house and I heard you go up the stairs to the apartment. When you didn't come back I followed. I found you sulking in the chair. I tried to cheer you up but you snapped at me so I told you I was leaving.

When I got across the room you ran and jumped on my back. You felt so light. I shrugged you off and turned. You slipped and I caught you in my arms. I could feel the strength of your lithe body. Our faces were closer than they had ever been. I leaned in and kissed you impulsively. I felt your body relax completely in my arms and you kissed me back. My mind was racing. *What are we doing? What does this mean? Have I destroyed everything?*

However, we kept kissing with deeper passion until we collapsed onto the floor. We never stopped. If you wanted to, you didn't say anything. You yielded to me. But I remember how you started to cry afterwards and I was scared.

"Go home." I don't want you to see me cry." And so I did.

That evening after my baseball game, when I came out of the shower there was an instant message from you.

"I need you."

"I'm on my way."

"No, meet me at the pool house at midnight."

"Okay, but I'll have to sneak out."

I was late that night because Conor was still at the house using Dad's law library and he caught me leaving. I never told you why then and you didn't ask. I had to convince him not to tell Dad and it took a while.

When I got to the pool house you looked worried. You didn't speak a word but pressed your body into mine and I held you. We never said much – we just spoke with our actions. We went upstairs to the apartment and slept together. Again you cried, but you didn't send me away. I was confused and depressed. I tried to comfort you and we fell asleep. I woke at 5:00 AM, nudged you so you could go back to your room. We kissed and I left. We were one Isa and it did not feel at all like a movie or a novel said it would. It was beautiful in a deeply melancholy way. And so it remains to this day.

After we became intimate, it was like a switch was thrown in my head. I could not stop thinking about you. The feelings were so strong that there are no words that can express it. I was hungry for you and when we were alone I could not keep my hands off you. Something changed inside and I was driven by raw emotion. When we were swimming I would stare at your body moving through water and it made me mad with desire. Inside my emotions were raging. I would chase after you and you would squeal. How did your mom not know? Did she just turn a blind eye?

When we danced I completely lost myself. Sometimes I would pick you up in my arms and spin. We were so happy. Did I just imagine this?

On the nights I could not sneak out we would chat online and you would torture me with sexual innuendo. I threatened to send it to your mom and you got angry. Even writing this now makes me smile. Our intimacy grew deeper and you no longer cried and I felt less responsible; but the melancholy stayed, the sense that all had fallen down.

In my mind, I was making plans for the fall when we returned to school. It was shallow, but I imagined how cool everyone thought I would be with you as my girlfriend. This is how thirteen-year-old boys think - but we never touched the fall together. I remember the day you told me you were moving. It was in the heat of the day and we were half asleep on the day bed. Your face changed and I knew something was wrong. You told me you needed me to be strong because you couldn't be. It made no sense; my strength was an act. I thought you could see through me.

You said, "We are moving to San Francisco. The movers are coming in three days and we are flying out that afternoon."

You studied my face for a reaction but I was in shock and my face was like stone. You said, "Please don't be angry."

I stood up and pulled on my T-shirt. You said, "Please don't cry."

I remember my exact words because they were the only words I could speak. "Why did you wait to tell me?"

I didn't stay for you to answer me, leaving as quickly as I could. Did you call after me? I can't remember. I was trying to control the anguish that was building in my body.

I avoided you the next day. I shut off my computer. I couldn't bring myself to see you or say good-bye. The night before you left was the only time I tried to see you. I snuck out of the house and walked down the street. I started toward your bedroom window. I heard shouting in Spanish and through the giant, picture window, I could see you were arguing with your father. I saw you burst into tears and run away. I turned and went home. You hated it when I saw you cry.

The morning you left, I awoke in disbelief. I sat around watching television, trying to distract myself. When I heard a car start, I ran from the house and down the street. A cab was backing up and you turned and looked at me. My love was drowning in your tears, our future running down your cheeks. We belonged together but they cut you from my soul and took you away.

You left the world we shared and I returned to the one I came from, where despondence waited to greet me like an old friend. I went home, my mind racing in disbelief that you were really gone. I went into my room sat on the floor and cried for the last time in my life. The whole week passed like a dream. I was dark as death; I could barely speak. I could not escape my thoughts. My mind raced in a million directions and nothing made sense. I lay down and slept to quiet my mind. I slept through the morning. I slept into the evening. My mother thought I was ill. I never said a word.

Two days after you left, I sat down and wrote you a letter so you would have something to keep. I sent it and I waited for an answer. The next week I sent another letter. I knew I did something wrong. I shouldn't have stayed away the last two days. I should have taken you into my arms and embraced you for the last time. I was so young I didn't know how to say good-bye or control my emotions. I tried to reach you on chat but you were offline.

The month after you left, my whole family went to Ireland to see my grandparents. Grandma could tell that I was sad, so she cajoled Grandpa into taking me fly fishing in *Loch Luíoch* in county Kerry. I picked up a postcard there and wrote you a short note trying to pretend things were normal. I forgot what I was doing and mailed it to your old address.

For a short time I put you out of my mind. We had to speak Gaelic the whole time we were there. This sounds strange, but not speaking English helped me deal with the separation. It was like it happened to someone else.

It was hard coming home. I went through all the mail, my email and there was nothing. Months passed; I overheard a high school girl say to her friend that she just didn't feel safe with her boyfriend and that's why she broke up with him. I thought that was the reason you wouldn't answer me. I never made you feel secure. One year later, I sent that stupid letter bragging about how tough I had become. I was a fool.

I have never forgotten your beautiful face. I can never forget the softness of your lips, the smoothness of your skin and the sense of belonging I had with you. I don't tell you this to make you feel bad. I am dying from possibly untreatable TB; I want to let you know how much you meant to me and how hard it was to learn to let go. Some sorrows are silent to us. Released from our hand they leave their mark unseen by us and felt by others. I know I hurt others. It is the way of the world.

I could have married you; I believe we would have been happy. If you had trusted me to lead, I would have found a way. This is not some idle romantic thought near death but the beauty of oneness between a man and a woman. We are born longing for transcendence. Melded together and bound in the dawn of love, we could have grown old together, spending our days on the routine things and never noticing the lines growing on our faces. We would have been each other's first and last. I now truly believe that is the way it is supposed to be. We wait too long to marry and just accumulate scars. I cannot help but think of a line from Verlaine, the poem, *Voeu*, which you loved for me to read to you in my terrible French: "*Sont-elles assez loin toutes ces allégresses. Et toutes ces candeurs!*"

The last weeks of reflection upon my life and my prior futile attempts at love have drawn me back to that point in time when I was in love with you. I have tried repeatedly to match what we had but I have failed. There are women for whom I have felt unrestrained passion. But only with you did I feel passion, friendship, acceptance and love. Words do not express the deep connection I had to you.

I searched the Internet for you but it returned too many responses. I hope you're happy, Isa. Even as I babble today in maudlin words and subjunctive thoughts, I hope you are satisfied in the soothing pace of the quotidian, as am I in the measured pace of my decline.

Two nights ago, not long after I began to compose this, I dreamed you came to see me. You lifted the coins from my eyes and kissed my brow like you did when we lay together. I smiled and struggled to rise but I couldn't. I realized I was dead.

There is a selfish part of me that wishes you had written to say there was no hope for us instead of the lonely silence. In the end it does not matter. I feel compelled to write what I feel, regardless of whether this letter ever reaches you. Perhaps you remember none, or only part, of what I have written here. Perhaps I was just a kid you knew once. I may never know one way or the other. They say I am a few weeks from death if I don't respond to the new treatment. My mind clings to life and the body decays. Is it better to have never known love than to see it disappear? Holding onto you was like trying to hold the breeze at nautical twilight. These words are for you, Isabel, the outpouring of my soul.

DECADENCE

January, Saint Louis

Marie, *Kleines,* we met on a directionless walk between listlessness and pleasure. Your family blamed me for what happened. I did not leave from the guilt, I left because it was finished. I left as an act of restoration. In the end, everyone got what they wanted in some bizarre way — including me, I suppose. (Although, as I sit and write this, it does not feel that way.) You were more than willing to sing with the chorus of supporters around you who treated you like a victim. That you were nothing but a hapless victim is a lie, a rationalization to avoid responsibility for your actions that disgusts me even now. If it feels like I am scolding you like child, it is because you deserve it. You always had the choice to just break up instead of playing a malicious game. Your father, that *Schlawiner,* used our unwinding as an excuse to extract a "loan" to cover his bad investments while assuming a posture of moral superiority. It was too much for me to take. In his mind, I purchased an indulgence for my sins against his daughter, as if being a woman made you free from moral responsibility. Your father is not the Pope. It is God in Christ who forgives sins and no one can purchase that. Does it surprise you that the man who left you as an atheist now is a Christian? Suffering and facing death ends superficial thinking. The Christian worldview predicted my life long before I was born.

Perhaps some day, in a moment of clarity, you will see the face behind the face was not as ugly as you were told. If I have learned anything from my mistakes, it is that hedonic pursuits are emasculating; they made me soft, corrupt – and I was less a man because of it. I made an agreement with your father and part of that was to leave Europe. This simple act restored things to what they once were. Whether that is useful or desirable, I leave you to decide.

I approached dark with desire when I saw you standing at the gate of your distant cousin's *Schloss* in Birstein, a beautiful place where we would spend a truly memorable evening listening to the Brandenburg Concertos 1 & 2. I still laugh about the piccolo trumpet player, that *ungeheuer* lesbian, holding her small trumpet in her chubby fingers and staring salaciously at you while she played. That was our innocent time together when everything was normal, when we were just getting to know each other. When our world together was joyous, before our passion consumed us, turning everything dross.

That first time I saw you I knew I had to meet you. There was vulnerability in your eyes; it is gone now. I took it away and gave you experience. I hate myself for that. Was I given life to destroy what is beautiful, to leave flowers to die in the desert? I did the thing I despised in others.

I received the three emails you sent to me nine months after you sent them. I was in prison for almost year in South Africa, jailed as an illegal immigrant. By then you were finished with me. The anger in your first email was misplaced; I gave you and your family what all of you wanted. The sorrow, regret and pleading in your second cut me to my core but it was too late for me to respond. I am less because of it. If there was any hope to start over, it died as I rotted in jail without due process. I hope you are happy now with Michael. He is from your class and culture, as you so carefully stressed in the final email. I know those things are important to your family. If it is any consolation, the man who hurt you is seriously ill and may die. For a brief time, we were consumed by 19th Century literature. How ironic is it that a 19th Century disease is consuming me? The bitter irony of dying from a "romantic disease" is not lost on me. I can laugh about it between coughing jags and detestable, periodic fits of self-pity. You can call me Violetto.

I told everyone after I graduated from the university, I was moving to Germany to study the language and philosophy. I lied. I came to the land of my grandfather's ancestors to die. Is that why we found each other? After I met you I wanted to make Germany my home, but I learned once again I have no home. What was Germany but one more place I had to leave? That day at the gate when I first spoke to you, you were wearing a formal dress and three-inch heels. It was rare to have a woman look straight into my eyes. How beautiful you were that night; I wanted you then. It took everything I had not to attempt to kiss you.

I remember you tried to get me to go away that first night with petty insults. Do you remember what you said? You told me I had one of those awful American accents. But I knew you were only trying to scare me off. I stared deep into your eyes. Your pupils were dilated every time I held them with mine and that told me everything. You continued to try to make me leave but you complied with my every request. I dominated you with my mere presence and you surrendered a millimeter at a time.

"Shhhh, it's time for you to stop talking." I shocked you, but you did.

"Take my arm." And you did. I walked you back to the door so you could return to the party. I said that you should come to Gelnhausen on Saturday for the *Altstadtfest* and meet me in front of the *Rathaus.* You did. I wish you had not. I wish, like so many girls, you would have just not shown up.

You came with your friend Sarah and we walked around and talked and drank wine. It was wonderful until the drunken volunteer firefighter wouldn't leave Sarah alone. Sarah tried only speaking to him in her native French but that seemed to only encourage his stupidity. In truth, he did not slip on the cobblestones and knock his head like I said. When you and Sarah turned to look at an arguing couple, I tripped him by stepping on his foot and then pretended to try to catch him. He got the message.

I invited you and Sarah back to my apartment in the *Obermarkt* for coffee. It was deliberate and calculated to move you one step closer to sleeping with me. I was setting you up in small stages, patient as a predator. My first motive was to use you. This is why you should be happy I am gone from your life. You deserved better.

I remember how impressed you were with the apartment; you didn't expect an American "to have an apartment like this." Like so many Germans, you assumed low taste in all Americans, as if 98 percent of us fall drunk out of the trailer every morning while snapping our pants. Don't smile, you know it's true.

We never had that coffee. Instead, we drank a bottle of wine. Your nervous friend Sarah wanted to drive back to Frankfurt but I convinced you to stay because it was dangerous to drive. You both knew I was right. I gave you and Sarah some blankets and then I went to bed. Later you said to me, "A gentlemen would have given us his bed."

I replied, "That's by invitation only."

The next morning I got up early and started to make coffee. I was standing in the kitchen, shirtless, pouring the water and when I turned around you were awake and sitting in the club chair watching me. I pulled on a shirt and apologized. You smiled and said good morning with the superior air you could affect. I cooked breakfast for you and Sarah. I liked cooking; it was a way of showing affection for others without ever touching them physically. Marie, you were so naturally affectionate. *Du fehlst mir.*

After breakfast I walked you both downstairs to the front door. It was cold for May when I opened the door and you didn't have a coat. I went back upstairs and brought two sweaters down. I wanted an excuse to see you again. I think you wanted one too. I said good-bye as you walked down the cobblestones. I heard Sarah say quietly, "I don't trust him, typical arrogant American."

And when she finished the remark you turned, ran back and

kissed me on the cheek. Lowering your head slightly you said *"Danke."* I wanted to carry you back up those stairs but I only muttered, *"Bitte."* For brief moment I watched the beautiful movement of your long legs and the wind lift your dark brown hair and make it dance. It reminded me of something from my childhood. I went inside and back to sleep.

When I woke up my phone was buzzing. You sent me a text. I've always wondered how you got my phone number.

Your message read, `"Coffee, Bad Orb, 4:30?"`

If you remember it was raining... again. I texted you back later in the day.

`"It's raining. I have a motorcycle"`
`"It's clearing soon. It will be sunny by then."`
`"Okay"`
`"See you there?"`
`"Maybe"`
`"Don't be boring."`
`"Okay"`

I arrived late, as you well know, sitting there with Sarah and your friend Oliver at the café drinking a coffee and eating cake. I walked up slowly to the table and I could see the surprise in your eyes that I arrived. You seemed pleased. I know why you invited me and why Oliver was there. You wanted a man's opinion. Who is this *Ami*? But your mind was already made up. You had decided in the first three seconds we met. I was already inside your mind and you were replaying every moment. This is not just my ego.

You could not hide your attraction. I could feel it in my body and I could see the warmth in your face and neck, your blushing subtle and constant when I stared at you. Your pale white skin told me the truth no matter how indifferent you sounded. There was something about you, your height, your body, the way you walked, your voice like fine emery paper drove me mad. Even then in our earliest meetings I wanted to take you in my arms and force a kiss upon you. I am conflicted even as I write this because I feel a deep sense of guilt over what transpired. I feel like I used you, that I wasted a year of your life but I also feel it's exactly what you wanted. There is a part of me that wants to start again —even though that opportunity has passed. I cannot help but wonder what it would have been like if we had taken more time in the beginning to know each other fully before the pleasures of sex clouded our minds. Still, today, *Ich habe so eine Sehnsucht nach dir.*

I remember Oliver played the class game by asking me

questions about my family background, the occupations of my father and grandfather, my last name, where we came from in Germany, and when we left. I didn't realize what he was doing until you told me later. Old families are meaningless to Americans unless they have held onto their money. In Europe, one always has their family name even if they don't have money. And, as I was to find out when my family line was checked, it was sufficient to receive unsolicited invitations.

I paid for everyone because, though we were all students, I had sufficient income from my trust and investments. You never told me what Oliver said but I am sure it was pejorative. He was, after all, German, from a "good family," and in his case that meant being critical of everyone and everything while shamelessly sponging off others and feeling superior. He was in love with you, but I think you knew that. At the end, he came to Gelnhausen to lecture me. I punched him in the face. It wasn't easy with a broken collarbone. If you see him, apologize for me. I hope he gets along with Michael.

After coffee, I walked with you and your friends back to your car. Along the way we ran into three different girls I knew. It seemed like the whole *Main-Kinzig-Kreis* was there. Your irritation was palpable, especially when Katya gave me a big hug and asked me where I had been hiding, that I should call her. I took her new phone number. You said to me in English, the first time I heard you speak it, "I see you are a very friendly boy." That made me smile.

A few steps later you caught your heel in the cobblestone and your shoe came off. You rested your hand on my shoulder to steady yourself while you put it back on. I gave you my arm until we cleared the cobblestones, after which I dropped my arm so you would let go and I moved away from you. You seemed surprised that I did that. I wanted to let you know how easy it was to walk away from someone as beautiful as you. You are so beautiful that modeling would have been condescension. No static picture could capture the entirety of your beauty and intelligence, even if you cannot see it. The simple fact is I did not fall into the trap of treating you better simply because you are beautiful. There had to be more to keep my interest.

We said good-bye at that point and we didn't see each other until Friday. Actually, I was surprised to see you in that club Friday night because it didn't seem like your style. I saw you from behind and did not recognize you in jeans. I was with friends from the university. I had a lot of those because they liked to drink for free. *Pecunia non olet,* even for the Greens.

I was speaking with my friend Ana when you noticed me. Your face changed completely. It was like you were angry because I hadn't asked you out again. I know that look well. A woman cannot hide it. In my mind, it wasn't time and things were on my schedule. That was the night the schedule broke. The whole that is you, your person, appearance, essence, the elegance and beauty that are you ended my plans. When our eyes met I smiled but I did not come over and your pride froze you.

I ran into Sarah coming back from the bar and she was friendly. I know she didn't like Americans but her manners were impeccable. While I was talking to her you came over and we started to flirt. You tried to get me to dance but I rarely did. It brought back bad memories. At some point you stood on your tiptoes while I was leaning back and in plaintive tones whispered in my ear in English, "Dance with me. I will dance for you."

It was a gift to see you move. A gift I keep forever in my mind; one that I cannot replace. As I danced with you it opened up feelings I had buried. I saw the happiness in your eyes, the joy of your movements and my plans ended. I connected to emotions I simply no longer wanted to feel. As I write these words the emotions return, the unwelcome guest pulling me down into the shadows. I cannot escape the memories. I shall never know again the purity of your movements and softness of your lips.. It feels so pointless to continue writing I am just torturing myself. I wish this were over. I wish I were dead.

§

It is the next day. This illness makes me weak, physically, mentally and emotionally but I cannot take back my words. The truth remains; all my planning and machinations were mere existence, the simple passage of time. The time with you was not. The way it started was simple enough. Wasn't it? We danced that night and left together. I had taken the train and you drove me home. I asked you up to my apartment but you refused. I got out and walked around to the driver's side. When I went to kiss you, you turned your head like it was just a big joke. I laughed, reached in the car and pulled you out through the driver's side window. You were laughing, half fighting me. Then we paused and looked at each other in silence. I was right up against you and I started to kiss you and you moved your head back again. This time I put my arms around you and kissed you forcefully. You kissed me back, revealing an intensity that would never be obvious to anyone who knew you. As quickly as it began it ended.

I pulled back and said, "Go home before I drag you upstairs."

Your lips were slightly tumid, the most alluring Cupid's bow I have ever seen. I opened the car door for you; we kissed briefly and you went home. I walked up the stairs to my apartment with the ghosts of the evening swimming in my mind. Emotions were fusing and I was fighting to keep control. The passion for you was building and I was hungry for the softness and affection only a woman can give. Not all women. Only you my Marie, only you.

I woke up with the phone vibrating on my nightstand. It was 6:00 AM and you were already awake. I don't know how you did it. If you hadn't texted me I would have stayed in bed for another couple hours. I recall your message was something like this.

"I have a huge bruise on my hip from last night!!!!!"

I texted you back. "Really? You should be more careful."

"You owe me. I will have to think of something special."

"Okay, you win, you can see me again."

"Haha, that's not what I meant."

"I'd say that was pretty special."

"Maybe for a puppy!"

"Don't be so hard on yourself. I don't think of you that way." Then I put down my phone and made coffee. After I had reviewed the markets, I picked up my phone. One of your messages caught my eye. "Do you have a dinner jacket or tux?"

"No."

"You'll need one. I'm taking you to a semi-formal dinner and concert tonight at Schloss Birstein. It's for charity."

"I see."

"Don't move I'm on my way. The only way we can do this in time is we go to a clothier my family uses."

About thirty minutes later you showed up and I got behind the wheel. "What time do they close today?"

"1:00 PM but they will need at least an hour to tailor it properly"

I insisted on driving because in my estimation it was the only way we were going to make it on time. The whole time I was driving, your right foot was working the invisible brake on the passenger's side. You were a nervous wreck but we made it on time. That day was so much fun. Sitting inches off the bumper of another car at 260 KPH focuses the mind.

We grabbed lunch afterwards and I teased you mercilessly about the ride into Frankfurt. Time got away from us, didn't it? It always did. I had you drop me at the main train station so you would have time to get ready.

We somehow managed in a mad rush to have me fitted in semi-formal clothes (you taught me that; true semi-formal is black tie.) I learned all the old traditions from you. Do you remember how worried you were that I would make errors around table manners and protocol? On the way there, you kept reminding me of things I had already learned in my childhood. I can smile now but back then, I was getting angry. It was funny how, as the only American at the table, people watched me all through dinner.

There are two things I remember most about the charity dinner (besides the piccolo trumpet player). One was how deeply affected you were by the music. Beneath that confidence was a young woman moved by beauty in a way that she could not hide. I looked over and there were tears streaming down your face. You were far more sensitive then you pretended. We are the same.

The other was the table conversation. Afterward, I could tell you were impressed because when we left the table you slipped your arm in mine as way of claiming me. With you on my arm, I felt like the luckiest man on Earth.

§

I am staring out of the window in my isolation room. They have taken respiratory isolation precautions because it appears I have XDR-TB. In other words, they are going pump me with a lot of different drugs to try to stop it. I don't care if I live or die. It is inconsequential to me. I don't belong or fit into the scheme of things. You know that better than anyone. It is human nature that if there was only one person on the planet who could provide you with everything that you crave in this life, it would be the only person from whom you do not want it from.

I am watching two teens, maybe fifteen or sixteen, walking along together from my window. You can tell they are boyfriend and girlfriend, even though they are not touching each other. The girl has a thin nose with a little bump at the top. It reminds me of you. The boy looks so proud, so confident. That's how I felt with you when things were still good -invincible.

Being your boyfriend was difficult because all the drunks would try to approach you if I wasn't there. Sometimes it took advanced levels of persuasion to get them stop, like a fist in the face. I know that made you angry. In your mind this was typical "American," but you felt safe.

I remember when you and your friends wanted to try hashish. It was against my better judgment but we went into an Irish pub to talk to a friend of mine, the bartender, Sean. He was into that sort of thing. I surprised you when we held the entire conversation in Gaelic. You knew so little about me and I didn't volunteer.

He set up a buy with some Turks but warned me to be careful. We met them in an alley in Sachsenhausen. That idiot Ernst accused them of trying to cheat us, and one of them pulled a 9mm pistol. I put you behind me and stood directly in front of it. Your friends panicked and ran. You stood behind me until I told you to run. I talked him out shooting me but not out of taking the money. I took the train home and turned off my phone because I was fully pissed off. When I turned my phone on I had three voice mails and twenty texts from you. I texted you back to say I was home and okay. You called me and got angry for making you worry and hung up on me. We didn't talk again until I got sick.

Shortly after that incident I got influenza. I had a 40-degree temperature. I was so sick I couldn't get out bed. I was getting dehydrated and started having wild hallucinations. I resigned myself to dying at that point. I still don't know why you stopped by or why I left my front door open. Were you expecting to find me with another girl? I am grateful you came. You saved my life. You slept on the couch and looked after me the whole weekend. Thank you. It was one of the kindest things anyone has ever done for me.

You left quietly early Monday morning after feeding me breakfast. You kissed me on the cheek just before you left and I could only mumble a feeble thank-you. I remember that because my fever had finally broken and I was starting to return to normal.

I was so weak after that I really didn't feel like going out. I texted you a couple of times to see if you wanted to just hang out at the apartment. You said no, so I just stopped texting you. I learned to stop thinking any one woman was irreplaceable when I was thirteen.

I texted Katya instead and she came over. Despite what you thought then, we were never more than friends. I helped her with an abusive boyfriend by pretending to be her new one. She was like a little sister to me. You said she wanted to be more than a friend and that you could tell. It didn't matter what she wanted. It only mattered what I wanted, and she was my friend. Besides, I wasn't too keen on red hair.

I was surprised to find you pressing the buzzer on my apartment in the middle of the week at 11:30 PM. I let you in and you glared at Katya. I can still see you sitting in the club chair, one leg crossed over the other, bouncing in irritation. I offered you tea and you refused. Every question anyone asked you, you returned with a curt answer like a bratty child.

I was going to send you home, but instead Katya had enough and left. No sooner did the downstairs door close when you started yelling at me so fast in German I couldn't understand you. I am sure you remember. It was the first time I saw you like that. I let you vent but I did not explain or apologize. It wasn't my way. I knew the truth and that's all that mattered. You were hurling accusations at me, like how many people was I seeing? and is this how I treat women?

Do you remember what I said? "Where did you get the idea that I was only seeing you? Did we make some kind of commitment that I missed? We've been out five times. You have ignored my every text for the last three days."

You answered, "Do you think I am some cheap prostitute that you just text to come over to your apartment?"

Then you started crying. I felt bad. I know that you thought I was playing a game but I wasn't. I just did what I wanted and it felt like a game to you. When one is conflicted they are sending mixed signals. I was hot and cold on you, on my education and life in general. I was financially secure because of my parents; I was doing really well with my investments - more luck than skill - but my emotional life was like a feather in the wind. I hid it well behind the mask of indifference.

I held you in my arms and did my pathetic best to reassure you. I don't know why I started telling you there was no one but you and I was going to take care of you but I did. After I said it, I realized what a self-serving liar I had become. You brought my conscience back from its deep torpor. I kept my word to you Marie. I never cheated on you. I gave you my word and, despite your suspicions, there was no one else but you. I took the blame at the end and only you knew the truth.

We sat on the couch and I put my arm around you and you laid your head on my shoulder. We fell asleep. At 2:30 AM I woke you and asked you if you wanted to stay with me or go home. You texted your roommate and stayed.

You woke me five hours later with a cup of coffee. I was still feeling run down by the flu. Did you wonder why I never made a pass at you that night? I was exhausted. It had crossed my mind. In fact, it was always on my mind but my body needed rest. It's funny how this moment and that one parallel each other. When we are sick, our desire is to be whole again. All other desires are diminished.

It was that morning when I kissed you good-bye that I began to realize you were an ingénue hiding behind your education and class. You knew much, but you did not have the experience. Your nervousness around me was your fear of what I knew and what I had done in the past. Your schoolgirl jealousy came from the fear that no matter how much male attention you had previously, you wanted mine and feared being less loved. You denied being a virgin but I know you lied to me. I do not understand the desire to hide it. Virginity has been valued in all cultures across the history of man. Today, it appears to be transformed into an inverse scarlet A, a mark of shame to be dispensed with as quickly as possible. I may be the last romantic on the planet, the last one who really cares, but I find it incredibly beautiful. I am less a man, less a human because things did not work out between us. I am equally saddened that you permitted them to bully you into turning on me. I was never your enemy.

I ask myself: why do we do what we do? The pleasure we imagine from any course of action is never matched by the reality; the imperfect follows the perfect. We start from the beautiful and degrade to the common.

After you left that morning we started seeing each other all the time, remember? It was peaceful. I was finishing my master's thesis and you were studying for your finals. I remember how disciplined you were in your studies. I remember you corrected my writing, fixing all my German grammatical errors. You didn't like philosophy so I know how painful it must have been. It was during that time I told you what a great, patient teacher you were and one day you would make a wonderful mother. You blushed Marie. It was true then. It is true today. You said you didn't want children. Like so many German women you wanted to finish your degree, start a career, travel and live for yourself. Do you still feel the same?

It was a relief to finish and get my master's degree. I was happy you came to the commencement ceremonies since my brothers couldn't. You asked me for the first time about my parents but I was evasive then and I just mentioned they had passed. We went out dancing with friends to celebrate. It was then I got the idea of going to a different club every night for a week. We really did nothing during the day. We went shopping and I bought you a lot of new clothes. You seemed to enjoy that. We talked a lot or, I should say,]]]] you did. I learned a lot about German culture and history from you.

The first night out I tried to get you to come home with me but you made an excuse about having to get up early and meet your father for breakfast since he was flying from Zürich to Berlin and wanted to stop in Frankfurt to see you. I thought nothing of it. On the second night your reasons for going home were less transparent. On the third night the club we went to was exclusively gay and you were the only woman there. We danced anyway but I only danced with you, despite the invitations I received. Again, I took you home.

On the fourth night we were in Darmstadt. When I came back from the bar there was a drunk hitting on you. Normally they would leave after awhile, but he wouldn't. You may remember it differently than I. You insisted you could handle the situation but I was getting angry. When he grabbed you around the waist from behind and tried to kiss your cheek, I got tunnel vision. I don't recall how many times I hit him but it was enough that he went down. I grabbed your hand to leave because I knew the bouncers would be on their way over and I didn't want any more trouble. We were almost to the door when one of them caught up to us. He seemed to think I was dragging you out against your will and got between us. He started pushing me out the door.

You never listened to my side of the story and that video that showed up on YouTube just showed the fight, so I will explain it to you from my perspective. I was willing to let it go and wait for you to come outside. I let the bouncer push me out the front door and I didn't resist. He was just doing his job. The doorman wasn't happy with that and decided to kick me in the butt for good measure. You were still inside. When he did that, I turned around to face him and the bouncer tried to sucker punch me but I got my elbow up and he hit that instead. He bent over holding his hand in pain. You walked out as I kneed him in the jaw and knocked him out. You started yelling at me to stop but the doorman was already punching me landing shots to my head and face. I spun to try to hit him with a reverse elbow and he ducked right into it knocking him down. I finished him with a knee too. By then you were begging me to stop and crying.

I yelled at you in English, "Let's go before the police get here." I did not want to be arrested and deported for assault. It was a chilly ride back to your apartment. You got out and slammed the car door and went straight into the building. I got my helmet out of the trunk, climbed on my motorcycle, and went back to Gelnhausen with your car keys in my pocket.

You texted me the next morning to ask about your keys. I didn't respond; instead I rode into Frankfurt. I texted you when I was outside and you came out. I handed them to you without a word, started my bike and left. I didn't even take my helmet off.

In your last letter you said even when I was wrong I made you feel like it was your fault. I was the counterfactual to every feminist fairytale told to you by our weak and rotting culture. I do not apologize for protecting those I love. Men who don't listen must feel. We get the behavior we tolerate. I guarantee both of those bouncers will think twice before they pull what they did on me. I guarantee the lecherous drunk, with his broken nose, will think twice before he puts his arms around another man's girl.

Night four was the end of our club hopping. We didn't go out that night and full day passed before we even communicated. I decided I wanted to cook for you so I texted you, "*Put on a beautiful dress, be at my apartment at 7:30 PM. I am going to cook dinner for you.*"

I think you thought that I was through with you because when you texted back you said, "*Are you sure???*"

I texted back, "*Bring a bottle of wine.*"

It was Saturday. We had been going out off and on for six weeks and I had barely kissed you. I couldn't believe it. German girls were so much slower than Americans but this was longer than I expected. Usually I would have lost interest by now but I hadn't. There was something that kept me waiting, something that kept me desiring you. The waiting was like torture.

When you arrived you looked amazing. You seemed pleased to see me wearing a sport coat and tie. I let you in and you handed me the bottle of wine. I gestured for you to follow me into the kitchen where I opened it. You were suspicious. You wanted to bring up the fight and my subsequent silence. I cut you off mid-sentence.

"Let's not talk about the past. Let's just enjoy the evening," is what I remember saying. Then I explained what I was cooking. I think it was venison ragout but I can't quite remember. I remember more my feelings that night.

I had peaceful jazz playing in the background. I was not trying to set a mood. I was trying to turn off the chatter in my mind. At some point I don't remember exactly when you grew playful again and started to tease me. You told me you were going to buy boxing headgear before we went dancing again in case I missed. That was a good one. Your change in mood was a welcome relief. It broke the tension.

At some point I asked you, "Do you feel safe with me?"

You answered, "Yes."

"Do you feel secure with me?"

"No," you replied, and changed the subject. I didn't really care at the time if you felt secure. I was too self-absorbed. It didn't seem to drive you away. The insecurity seemed to bring you closer to me. The more erratic I was the harder you tried to keep me happy. I think it just fed my ego.

I recall you drank two glasses of wine for each one I did. You even mentioned that you had never seen me drunk. I told you I didn't like who I was when I was drunk. You pressed me a bit. "Are you scary crazy when you're drunk?"

"No," I said, "I can get mean."

"Really?" You sounded incredulous and had a cynical smile on your face. "I will have to see that sometime."

You did, of course, at the end. It didn't turn out well did it? You should have taken me at my word.

We could talk about nearly anything, though we stayed away from politics. You might have been sympathetic to the CDU but you still had the German state paternalism attitude. "Americans talk about rights and Germans talk about responsibilities," you once said. An oversimplification but it had a kernel of truth. I made coffee and you had a Bailey's and I had a Cognac. When we finished we began to clear the table.

After we had put all the dishes in the dishwasher I went back to the table to get the bottle of cognac. When I looked at you, I saw you fully, as though for the first time. I saw the true Marie, not the superficial appearance or the first impression, but t he totality of who you are. The waves of desire began to wash over me like sheets of heavy rain. I was staring at you and you saw me; you could read my intent. You knew what was I was going to do when I began to walk to you. A flush ran across your face and you froze, staring at me. These details are etched into my memory. I kissed you and you felt passive in my arms but you returned my kiss like we would die tomorrow. We kissed for a long time and I kept escalating. Unlike before, you did not stop me. I picked you up and carried you to my bedroom. I remember you only said in an almost pleading tone in English, "Ryan, please," and then you laid your head on my shoulder and didn't say another word.

I did not know what you meant then. Now I do. I wish now I had controlled my own selfish desire but I am not the person today that I was then. Our sexual intimacy improved nothing emotionally. If anything, it did the opposite. Everything changed after that night. It always does. You became more self-confident. You attempted to control me, to dictate the pace and direction of our time together. I was not thinking rationally. When we were apart, I was consumed with seeing you again. When we were together, I could not keep my hands off you. My passion erased every flaw in our relationship. It clouded my judgment and yours.

Intimacy makes us believe in a fairytale that somehow things will just work.

At your worst, you competed with me constantly, even in minor things. It was if you wanted to lead but you couldn't; you knew only what you didn't want. I wish you had stopped trying to be my equal. The ways in which you were my better I listened to you. I took your advice. Your social abilities had no equal. But you would never be my equal. And yet you intruded, argued, and challenged me as if it were sport. I am stronger than you and you know that's true. It is not something someone gave me or something I earned or something I built over time. It is what I am. It is effortless. You wasted far too much emotional energy trying to prove otherwise. Your war was not against me but human nature. When things went bad at the Hotel Sacher, you suddenly became the victim under the spell of a sociopath. We have to really know someone well before we can treat them like trash. The courtesies reserved for the stranger disappear for those we love. We don't betray those we have met casually. We save that for those who love us.

At your best, you could make anyone feel good about themselves. When we were together I felt like a giant. You pushed me to stop being satisfied with things as they are, to set goals and look for challenges. Unfortunately, I wasn't able to stay and complete any of them. I learned to enjoy things I had long stopped caring about - literature and dance. You introduced me to a world that otherwise was invisible to an American expat, the intersection of the old aristocratic families and the wealthy.

That week it rained, the one before we set off on our trip, we just stayed at my place and read to each other. I liked doing that once when I was a young teen and I hadn't done it much since. I had all these books of late 19th Century authors and we started to read them. You found *"Confessions of an Opium Eater"* and we started reading. The English was difficult for you to understand and I found myself explaining what was going on. It was usually you who explained things to me. I missed subtleties in German and you helped me.

Marie, sometimes a thought arrives and it is just as quickly dismissed. The same thought arrives nestled in a new context, an ideal environment and it begins to feel attractive. The piece of coal in your hand starts to feel like a jewel. As I lay in bed with you and while you were sleeping, a feeling of emptiness encompassed me. Was it the result of sexual intimacy without commitment? I can't be sure but this much I know: at the point of maximum pleasure, I see the outline of something transcendent and all emotions blend into one. When I collapse, there is one feeling left, an elegiac taste. There was a glimpse of something perdurable but instead, I return to this world. I have never shared this with anyone. It may surprise you that I am willing to talk now. I am very ill, could possibly die and I suppose I don't really care if I admit weakness. What difference does it make? Facing death strips you of pretension.

When we were together, you continually probed to see my inner world. You stood outside, beating on the door relentlessly. When I finally let you into the antechamber and you saw the outline of my weakness, the edge of my vulnerability, you threw it back in my face in a moment of anger. You reached for the small leverage you had, that moment of honesty I shared with you. You betrayed my trust. I don't know what is worse: the betrayal or your assumption that it was a trivial matter. I think this medication is making me nauseated. I need rest.

§

I am going give you my recollection of our final weeks together. I feel I owe you an explanation. Your first letter was full of anger, confusion and errors. The trip started as a way to distract my mind. I was starting to feel a sense of purposelessness. I had no worries for money. I had my master's degree. I thought about getting a PhD. And yet, I needed change. I needed a distraction or I would fall back into the dark. I did not want you to see me this way. It had been more than a year since it happened last. Having money buys you freedom but if you don't know what to do with that freedom, then it has bought you nothing. I would rather be poor and have my parents alive.

Just after I arrived in Germany, before I started the master's program, and more than a year before we met, I became deeply depressed. The mood came upon me like it did after my parents died. So what I did was just climb on trains and drift. After a couple weeks, I was in Leipzig and stumbled on the *Wave Gotik Treffen*. At 3 AM, I was standing on a mostly empty train platform trying to make my way back to the hotel. I saw some drunken neo-Nazis and didn't think anything of it because they were around at the festival. Suddenly, I was blindsided. I stumbled and they started punching and kicking me. It wasn't going well. Out of the blue, another German entered the fight. He was really big, around 200 cm. I thought after he knocked down two of them they would be finished but they weren't. It was the most brutal fight of my life. Only my new friend (Karl-Heinz) and I walked away.

Two were unconscious and bleeding. One had his knee broken by Karl-Heinz, the fourth was sitting down trying to get back up but kept falling.

Karl-Heinz pushed me to leave and I followed him. He said we were most likely caught on surveillance cameras so we needed to leave quickly. He was on leave from the Foreign Legion and would be headed back to France later that morning. He told me to leave Leipzig just in case. We traded contact information. Life is funny, I ran into him two more times, that last night in Vienna (where you met him) and in Cape Town after I left Germany. What are the odds?

The strange part of the experience, even though I had a cracked rib and a broken nose, is that I pulled out of the malaise. The experience broke the cycle and I entered Goethe *Universistät* with a clear mind. It was my thinking that if we took off on the *Les Fleurs du Mal Summer Tour* (as you cynically called it), we could just be tourists, enjoy ourselves, and everything would pass. My other option was to level with you and just work through it. Somehow I didn't think you would find me particularly attractive if I admitted that. I cannot say even today if that isn't still true. Marie, I would have loved to lean against you for support but my instincts told me you would have moved away.

I proposed the idea that we spend time in different hotels and party continuously. I was set to receive a distribution from the trust and I saw no reason not to spend some of it since I had finished my master's degree and I was up for the year in my investments. We had big plans to live the next three weeks in five star hotels. You picked the cities where you had friends or family. Start in Frankfurt; go to Zürich to see your parents, then Salzburg, Vienna and finally Prague. We never made it to Prague.

In Frankfurt. you wanted to stay in the Intercontinental because it was near the river. While I wanted to stay in Hessischer Hof because it was authentic five star, I relented and we wound up in a junior suite at the Intercontinental. The first two days we barely left the bedroom. We just hung out the "do not disturb" sign and ordered food. We got a call from the front desk to make sure everything was okay. I think they wanted to get into the room to make sure we weren't trashing the place. On the last night there we threw a party and invited our friends from the university. Someone called security a couple of times for the noise but we eventually toned it down.

The next morning we still had a suite full of people but most were sleeping. I woke up in my clothes and you were next to me and Sarah (who was just back in town) was next to you. I'm glad she felt so comfortable. I got up and called the front desk, ordering breakfast for everyone. I remember some guy came up to me and asked, "Who is paying for all of this."

I pointed to a sleeping girl I didn't know and said, "She told me you were." You should have seen his face.

I woke everyone up who wasn't awake already. We had a nice breakfast and people started leaving. We debated whether to take the train to Zürich or drive. Fatigue won and we decided to take the train. We cut it close but we made it. On the way to Zürich, you explained to me for the first time that your father was an Honorary Consul and he was running the family business from there. You had to explain the position to me. I did not know it was unpaid.

I wasn't sure what to expect when we got to Zürich; it was early evening. I guess I was picturing an old mansion when the cab pulled up in front of an ultramodern home. You had me buy flowers for your mom as was the German custom. When she greeted us at the door she didn't smile until she discovered the flowers were for her. I think her incredulity was normal for a mother whose only daughter is bringing a man into her home for the first time. I was on my best behavior, standing whenever your mother entered the room. You told me that wasn't necessary but I continued until she told me to relax. I like your youngest brother; it was easy to relate to him. I was roughly the same at age fifteen. Your immediate younger brother, well, he was a *Schwulle*, sullen and sneered at everything. I have nothing more to say about him.

Your father got home later that night; I think it was around 9:00 PM. We were drinking wine. I saw where you got your height. He was about 3 cm taller than I. I stood and shook your father's hand. I looked him the directly in the eye. Your father had that slimy European way of asking questions that implied more than he was asking. There was a motive behind every question. Mark out certain words with tone and emphasis in any question to ambiguously imply curiosity, contempt or any combination thereof.

"So Ryan, Marie tells me you're an AMERican, hmmm?"

I know you are very close to him so there is no point in my criticizing him further. We did not like each other; that much is clear. I am sure he is happy I am gone. I will grant him this; he is a man of his word. He said he would make sure there were no charges pressed against me in Austria and he would obtain a one year renewable student visa for South Africa --once I made him the loan.

The night before we left for Salzburg, your father had a

business acquaintance and his wife for dinner. You did an amazing job of charming the two of them. You deftly steered the conversation around controversial subjects but kept things interesting. The man was clearly charmed by you. You are amazing. I realized that night I was falling in love with you. I didn't want to, it was just happening in tiny steps.

When the conversation rolled around to me, the inevitable question was, "What do you do?"

"I manage my own investments," I said.

I used to like saying that until I gave up the need to impress people. For a while I'd say "I'm a bartender" and see how they would treat me. These days I tell the truth. "I'm dying. That seems to occupy a lot of my time."

I was happy to leave Zürich and get far away your odious father, with his snide comments and insinuations. On the train to Salzburg, your opening comment was your mother's impression. "Strong silent type, something is hiding under the surface."

Next, your brothers. "He's not as American as I imagined he would be," and, "He's pretty cool." Then you got to your father. Really, I didn't want to hear it or care. I can't remember your words. After each criticism, you would study my face for a reaction. I think you expected me to defend myself. It wasn't worth the effort. What I recall your father saying is he didn't think I had a sense of direction or purpose - that I would spend my life going in circles regardless of how much money I had made. Of course, that didn't prevent him from helping himself to some of it.

The other thing he said was that and I was incapable of making you happy. That wasn't my responsibility. We are responsible for our own happiness.

I think a bit of his attitude affected you because you started asking questions like, "Why don't you pick a career?" and "How come you never talk about your family?" and "Why you are so evasive about how you feel?"

It was all very tedious. I might have answered you if the tone didn't sound like it came straight from your father. My one word and obtuse answers didn't satisfy you so you continued to press me. When I had enough I walked out the compartment and into second class. I sat down and struck up a conversation with two Austrian girls and started teasing them. They were laughing at the crazy American when you came looking for me. Your face changed immediately but you handled it well. You said you were having trouble with your laptop and needed my help.

When we got back to the compartment, I expected a fight but instead you really were having trouble with your laptop. I am smiling now. You handled that well. I never really knew what to expect with you. We are the same.

When I figured out the config error and had things working again, you said, "At some point you need to trust me." It didn't come up again for couple days. The last hour of the train ride we rode in silence. You were reading, I was reading, and the tension hung like a divider between us.

It was around 5:00 PM, I think, when we arrived at the Hotel Sacher. You said we would stay in the same hotel in Vienna. We checked in and you wanted to see the room. After we walked through the room, you weren't happy. You wanted one with a balcony overlooking the river. The clerk said that at least for that night they were occupied. Your faced changed completely and you snapped at the hotel clerk. You used your full name and title, which I had never heard you do before, and told him you wanted a room with a balcony. He looked annoyed but was polite.

When he returned he said he had a room for us but it was more per night. You told him not to worry, you would talk to the hotel manager. We visited that room and you were satisfied. After we had the luggage brought up, you turned to me and said, "We will get it at the same price as the other room. They should have recognized my name when the reservation was made."

"It was in my name," I said.

"Oh. Did you use von or just your last name?"

"Just my last name. My grandfather dropped the von."

"Next time use von. It carries more weight in Austria, at least in some circles."

It was early evening. I remember we went for a walk along the river. You decided to cross over and go to the *Getreidegaße*. You wanted to get a bottle of champagne, bread and pâté before the stores closed. It would be a nice walk and cost less than at the hotel. Just as we turned down the *Getreidegaße* I ran into an American I knew from college, Teresa. She was really excited to see a familiar face. She invited us to a party at the house she was staying in on the *Mönchsberg*.

You were less than thrilled with idea but with a little pressure you went along with it. If I recall your biggest concern is that there would be no one from your class and you would feel out of place. It didn't turn out that way, did it? You had friends who were also studying at the *Mozarteum* and they came to the party.

It was the first time you had met anyone from my past. Teresa told me later you were asking her what I was like during my undergraduate days. I don't think it was particularly satisfying for you, since we were really only acquaintances.

Someone was complaining about the heroin smuggling through Austria and out of the blue you announced that you wanted to try opium. You thought it would be an interesting experience. People around us sort of lightly laughed then everyone realized that you were serious. The ex-professional soccer player looked at you and said, "We need to see the Albanian. He can get it. Who has cash?"

You looked at me as if to say give him money. I raised my eyebrows and you said, "Come on, let's make this the *Les Fleur du Mal Summer Tour.*"

I remember everyone laughed then they started getting excited about the idea. The general feeling was, "Why not?"

I had never done drugs. It carried no fascination for me. I was on the spot and my ego got in the way of my judgment. I gave him the money. One poor decision begins a cascade, slow at first, then all at once.

Two hours later he returned with the opium. By that time, there were only about six of us left at the party. As I recall no one seemed to know exactly what to do since no one wanted to smoke it. Teresa looked it up on the Internet and said we should eat a 1/8 gram maximum so to be safe she cut that in half. She weighed it out in her kitchen scale and gave some to everyone. Then she said, "It may make you nauseated."

Thirty minutes later at least two people had vomited. The effects started slowly. At some point people became annoyed by the music. They kept changing the selection until they settled on *Bach: Goldberg Variations.* I sat down on the couch with you and watched you to see if you would get sick. It didn't seem to bother you. At some point our conversation ended and I looked around and everyone was sitting or lying down. There was just the music. I noticed for the first time in my life the chatter in my head was silent. I could focus on nearly anything I wanted without an intrusion. My body was fully relaxed and you were laying against me your head resting on my arm. I looked around the room again and everyone had their eyes closed. My body was relaxed and my mind was active. At some point I dozed off but I was aware of my dreams fully. They were wild, colorful and meaningless. Around 6:00 AM things had wound down. I got up, walked out of the Salon, and into the library. I saw the footballer sitting in a chair drinking coffee and reading a book.

"How was it?" he asked in British English.

"Different," I said. "How about you?"

"Didn't do it. I have no interest in that shit. It can't be good for you. Fresh coffee in the kitchen, mate."

"Thanks."

I went into the kitchen where you found me shortly thereafter. You came and snuggled up against me. You whispered in my ear, "I can still feel it in my body. It feels heavy. Let's go back to the hotel. I'll call a cab."

By the time the cab showed up on the *Mönchsberg*, everyone was awake and talking about the experience. Very few were interested in doing it again. That one student - Bernhard? -from the *Mozarteum* was really blown away by it and was ready to do it again. I started to give him what was left but you took it, cut off a piece and gave it to him. Then we went out to the waiting cab and back to the Hotel Sacher.

Back at the hotel we showered and went back to bed. I finally slept peacefully. You woke me with a kiss; that is truly a beautiful way to wake up. You laid your warm body against mine and placed your head on my chest. We clung to each other, flesh to flesh.

When I held you, I felt I could fight back the world. I would have done anything for you. As old as time, the instinct in man is to sacrifice for those whom he loves. I rolled over on top and kissed you. I let you feel the strength of my passion without speaking a word.

Later, after I had showered, I ordered lunch to the room. When I hung up the phone I felt completely different. In fact, at that point I felt everything was wrong. I can't explain why I felt that way. It just came upon me, the feeling first and then my mind tried to explain it, to give cause.

I remember I left the room and went for a walk along the river. I thought I could think it through and understand why I was starting to spiral down. I thought something was wrong between us. I felt lonely. The problem with loneliness is that even if you are with someone you care about deeply, it doesn't go away. You are just lonely with someone else around. I decided that the cause was within and not external to me. This thought brought me no satisfaction or peace, but I went back to the hotel.

You asked me when I got back where I went and I was evasive. Now you know. I did not tell you because I believed you would have thought less of me. Many women want the illusion of perfect strength in a man. There is no room for the flaw, the humanity or the crack in the stone.

We sat down to lunch and there were four to five letters on a tray. "What are those?" I asked you.

"Invitations to coffee or tea, most likely."

"Really, from whom?"

"One from the bishop, a new club opening, and someone I don't know. They must know my father, possibly my family name."

"Planning on going to any of them?"

"The bishop is an old family friend so I will have tea with him, that's for tomorrow afternoon. Don't worry, you don't have to go."

I remember saying at the time, "Why not meet with a religious dinosaur? They will disappear from the earth soon enough." How ironic that I am one of those dinosaurs now. You got up from table and came back with the opium and cut off two small pieces.

"We have no plans today. Let's see if this is different this time."

We dissolved it in our tea and I drank mine quickly. You drank it slowly. For a period of time I thought I was going to throw up but eventually it dissipated. We went out onto the balcony and sat in the chairs. It was cool but the sun was nice and warm. While we were talking about the beauty of the day, I felt a wave of warmth pass through my body. It was not intense. I suppose this was the diminished version of the "rush" a heroin addict feels before habituation sets in. I noticed there was periodic glimmer to the edges of objects. Again the internal chatter came to a halt. I reached over and held your hand. You looked back at me and smiled. We closed our eyes and just felt the sun's warmth. I had a general sense that everything was fine, a beautiful illusion.

I looked over at you again. Your eyes were closed. I saw the softness of your full lips. Your face was relaxed and I could detect the outline of your smooth, regular breathing. My eyes traced the outline of your lips up your thin nose across the small bump there that you hated. I wanted to get out of my chair and kiss your lips but for a time I was frozen and my mind wandered. Where was euphoria? Was it in this moment or the next? I know what you remember is the soft kiss I placed upon your lips and though nearly dead at first, you stirred and started kissing me back.

I led you to the bedroom, holding your hand; you were walking as if a great weight had been put upon you. I undressed you and you seemed passive - so opposite to the woman I knew. You did not resist me. As I made love to you, an opium dream swirled in my mind. I tried to transcribe it into a lyric poem. It was a visual display of what I was feeling at the time. I did not share it with you. It was a kind of prophecy. This is the poem.

Night becomes an ocean
Two lovers face-to-face

I'm falling from the sky
Still cold from empty days
The shadows from their smiles
Darken all my thoughts
Can you find a lover
In the crowd?

Euphoria
Where have you been?
I can hear your voice
I can't feel your hand

I have watched desire
Swallow all of life
The cross-world spiral
Strangles all delight.
Swimming for the silence
Melting into thought
Kissing on your lover
Inside the broken heart

§

Another full day has passed since I wrote last. I was too exhausted yesterday to type anything. If I live you won't see this anyway, so in a strange way, it's like talking to the wall.

When we woke after our final use of opium, it was dark outside. I think we were both stir crazy and hungry because we couldn't wait to get showered, changed and go out to dinner. It was there in that quite nearly empty restaurant, on my second glass of wine, when you asked me about my parents again. I think you roughly spoke these words: "You said your parents died in a plane crash. What happened?"

I was finally starting to trust you enough to open up and answered, "My dad was flying his plane back from a client meeting along Lake Michigan and Mom had gone with him. He ran into a sudden thunderstorm over Iowa and was unable to fly around it. He crashed trying to put it down in a farmer's field. I was seventeen."

You looked a little surprised when I said that and I saw sympathy in your eyes. You answered, "I'm sorry, it must have been hard on you."

I replied something along these lines, "I went to live with my oldest brother Declan who had just finished his residency as a surgeon. I said some things at the time about the futility of life and they put me on suicide watch in a psych ward for a month. It was total overreaction on their part. They put me on anti-depressants, which I hated. That's why I didn't really do drugs. It was long time ago and I have learned to live life like it's on a roller coaster; enjoy the high and get ready for the low. At least there is a breeze on the trip down."

You had a shocked look on your face and excused yourself. I rose for you as you left. When you came back, I could not say for sure, but I thought that you had been crying. I didn't ask. You didn't talk much more that evening. I talked a lot that night. I can't recall even about what.

The next day was just a regular day. We had tea with the bishop. You had to tell him that I was an atheist. He said one thing to me that stuck with me and eventually led to my rejection of atheism. He asked me, "Have you ever felt grateful? For anything at all, a beautiful day, friends, family?"

"Yes, of course," I replied.

"Why do you think that is? Gratitude takes an object."

I don't remember my answer. I used to have these pat answers; I suppose I pulled one of those out. His question stayed with me. I thought about it a long time. It haunted me from South Africa and back to the United States. Eventually, I decided there must be a God. If you ever see the bishop again, tell him I said thank you.

The next day we took the train to Vienna and checked into the Hotel Sacher. Do remember my last words before we left Salzburg? "Please get rid of the remaining opium before we leave."

When we checked in at the hotel, there were already invitations waiting for us at the front desk. It felt like I was in small town not the seat of the old Austro-Hungarian Empire. We had a beautiful room and a wonderful view of the first district. The first day there we visited the Cathedral and we walked to Der Demel for coffee and cake. The first district is an architectural museum and you were quick to point out all the different periods displayed there. You know so much about European history.

As we headed back to the hotel, I had no idea that in just one night, everything would be over. We got back and you weren't hungry and neither was I. You picked up the phone and ordered two bottles of champagne to the room. Then you announced, "We are going to drink both bottles."

"No, thanks."

You started to needle me. "What are you afraid of? Let's

celebrate our arrival here and have a good time."

And so, the bottles arrived and we started drinking the champagne. You were teasing me but it was little more aggressive than usual. The edge was a little harder. I was still sober then so I know my recollection is exact. At some point, the magic of the champagne went from light hearted to morose. I had stopped drinking but you pushed me to drink more and my judgment was already impaired so, in my way of thinking, you would get what you wanted whether the outcome was attractive or not. I know I should have stopped. Who started the ugly talk was it you or me? I don't recall.

The petty insults started over minor things. I do recall is at one point I commented that you had gained a few pounds on the trip, which wasn't true. I was being mean. Then you, in anger and hurt, blurted out, "I may have gained weight but no one ever had to stick me in the asylum."

It was dead silent for moment. I crossed the room toward you. What did I look like? You threw you hands up in front of your face and said, "Don't hit me."

I realized my fists were clenched. I turned and left the hotel room. When I did I realized how drunk I was, I turned to go back because I didn't want to be out in public that way. I went back to the hotel room but you had barred the door. I never touched you and you barred the door.

"Go away," you said, "I'm afraid of you."

"Come on. Let me in."

You didn't. I assumed at the time you were drunk like me. It wasn't until the morning that I realized you were pouring your champagne into the water pitcher.

I left and wandered the city. I found a club and went inside. It was midnight. I started looking to replace you. It was the way I dealt with the pain of fighting or breaking up. I just replaced the girl with someone else. I met these two Ukrainian girls, Yulia and Vira and started dancing with them. They wanted me to go with them to another club and I did. I stayed drunk for the first time in four years and the night passed in a blur. We went to other clubs and I cannot remember where I was. I remember being kind of mean to them and they just laughed. We were sitting in the back of the cab when I took out my phone and saw your text.

"Please come back."

Yulia leaned over and read it. She said something to her friend and they laughed. Then she took my phone and added her phone number to my address book. It was 4:30 AM. We went to one more place and then I put them in a cab and said good-night. I grabbed another cab and headed back to the hotel. My phone buzzed on the way back and it was another text from you. It was 6:00 AM.

"Where are you?   Are you okay?"
"Yes."

When I got to the hotel room, I was able to enter. I got undressed and climbed into bed. I turned my back on you. There was three feet and an infinite amount of space between us. I expected you to apologize but it never came. You took something I shared with you in trust and used it against me as a cheap, personal insult. I woke around 1:00 PM but you weren't around and I was relieved. I started to pack my things to leave but I changed my mind. It was a terrible mistake. I left and walked around the first district. I texted Yulia and met her for coffee at Demel's. I was already thinking past us but my heart was not in it. I wanted to be with you. Yulia talked and I listened. It was actually great to speak English, where I understood every word and every nuance.

I got back to the hotel around 5:30 PM. When I entered the room, you were reading or trying to. You were clearly annoyed. "Where were you?" you asked.

"I went the same place you did." That seemed to make you more upset. I was determined not to let your disapproval control me.

"I had lunch with an old friend,"

"Yeah, me too."

"He invited me ... us ... to a party. It's in the eighteenth district."

Isn't funny how we tell on ourselves? You were invited, not me. An old male friend. It's amazing how they just show up at the first sign of trouble. It's like if I could see inside your mind there are all these potential suitors lined up waiting to take their turn. I wasn't sure if you were trying to make me jealous. I brought up what you said the night before. I remember distinctly you laughed it off and told me, "Don't be so sensitive."

Marie, I knew in my core that we were finished. I couldn't share anything with you. If I did, it would come back to haunt me. I couldn't trust you. The sad thing is my passion continued to blind me. I couldn't trust you and yet, I did not want to let go. I wanted to get past this moment. Like tree roots at the bottom of a lake, sexual intimacy ensnares us. We grow desperate to leave but it holds us in place until we drown. I knew when I didn't leave earlier I was going to drown. I just didn't know how.

We went to the party and took a cab ride out to the house. It took about twenty minutes. We hardly spoke. The cab pulled up in front of this large mansion and we got out. Your "friend" met us at the door. He seemed surprised to see you with me so it was clear that you hadn't mentioned it before. He was taller than I was. Michael introduced himself and shook my hand. He held out his arm and you took it and he walked you into the party. I strolled in behind the two of you, fully enjoying the petty insult.

I looked around and saw a small bar and fetched us wine. When I started to hand it to you, you already had one. You just gave me a cynical smile. You were still holding Michael's arm. It was clear to me that we were through and yet I wouldn't accept it. It was nearly impossible to let go of what we had. Everything seemed to be slowing down. The ancient pain returned. Death is preferable to ever feeling that way again. If I die from TB, at least I will never again know the sorrow of everything unraveling; never again will I feel the knife thrust into my stomach and the fading smile of vindictiveness on a woman's face.

I turned my back on you - the only act I was capable of doing. I walked across the room, making my way through the throng of people. The first attractive women I saw without a drink, I approached without hesitation handing her the wine I had taken for you. "This has been waiting for you."

"Are you an American?"

I had my back to you. As I was talking to her, I felt this heavy hand on my shoulder and I turned to look and it was Karl-Heinz. I was amazed to see him there. He gave me a big smile.

"What are you doing here?" I asked.

"I should ask you the same question. I thought you might still be fighting skinheads in Leipzig."

"No, I came with my girlfriend. She is a friend of Michael's.

"Where is she?"

I pointed to you across the room. His face changed but he didn't say anything. He didn't need to.

"Yes, well, we rescued Michael and other members of an NGO in Chad last year. He told me if I was ever in Vienna he would throw a party, so here I am."

I introduced the girl I was speaking with to Karl-Heinz. She was suddenly interested in him. While the three of us were talking, I heard my name. I turned to look and it was Yulia. She came and gave me a big hug. I spun her slightly and when I did I saw the look on your face from across the room.

How long was it before you started the chain of events that brought things to an end? It couldn't have been more than ten minutes. We were all laughing at something Yulia said and I saw

Michael making a straight line for me, his chin jutting out. He walked up to me and said loudly in English, "I'm afraid I am going to have to ask you to leave."

It caught me by surprise. "Why?"

"Marie told me what happened last night. You need to go."

Again, I was surprised and confused. I composed myself. "What do you think happened?"

"Marie told me you grabbed her last night in drunken anger and threatened her."

At that point I smiled. I knew I was being set up. I knew you had crossed the final line. "Let's go talk to her we can straighten this out."

"No," he said, "you have to go now."

I stepped forward but Karl-Heinz rested his hand on my shoulder holding me back firmly but in a relaxed way. He leaned down and whispered, "There is no way this ends well. Just leave. It's best. Someone is playing a mean game here. Don't be a pawn."

I can still see the smug look on Michael's face, as if Karl-Heinz was his personal bodyguard. He had no idea. I didn't want to make a scene, so I handed him my wine glass turned and left. I cannot forget the look on your face. It went from satisfaction to worry.

I got outside and called a cab. Yulia showed up minutes later.

"What was that all about?"

"Well, I have been accused of assaulting my soon to be ex-girlfriend."

"Oh, is it true?"

"No, I think she is trying to get some cheap revenge for last night."

"You were with us."

"Yes, but we had an argument before that and I left the hotel. That's the extent of it."

"How much longer are you in Vienna?" she asked.

"I am leaving tonight."

"Oh," she said, "you have my number stay in touch." Then she gave me a weak smile and went inside.

My cab pulled up and I got in. I turned to look at the house and you were standing on the steps looking at me with tears in your eyes. There was the world we shared, the physical world we lived in. There was the secret world of unspoken thoughts, emotions and inference. The secret world blew up and spilled over into the one we occupied. As I looked at you my face like a stone, I thought that this was the end. But it was only going to get worse, thanks to Michael.

Here is what happened at the hotel, since we never spoke after that night. I got back to the room and started to pack. I thought I heard the door rattling so I walked toward it to investigate. The door flew open, striking me and breaking my collarbone. I slammed against the wall my head snapping back. I remember coming to in the hospital. They took me in for x-rays. There was policeman with me. He told me I was being charged with possession of opium. It was in my suitcase. I knew that was not accurate. If it was in any suitcase it had to be in yours. The doctor told me they were going to have to do surgery on my collarbone to repair it. It was going to be a couple of days before they could get it scheduled, so they put me in a room and handcuffed me.

On the second day of my arrest your father showed up. He said you had explained to him what happened. He offered me the deal. His "loan" was one quarter of my liquid net worth. I didn't care, really. I thought I could just make it up over time. I certainly did not want to face jail in Austria for something I didn't do.

After surgery and half day of recovery, the police escorted me to the train station and put me on the train. It was long, slow ride back to Frankfurt. I had to wait a couple of weeks before I could get my visa to South Africa. Your father took care of everything. I didn't even need to go to the consulate. I spent my last month in Germany shutting down my apartment and saying good-bye to friends.

I have a small steel plate and six screws on my collarbone. When I was on my way to South Africa I had to change planes in Madrid. I triggered the metal detector. I don't speak Spanish so it caused some delays and I had to run for my plane. If you want to have a good laugh, just think of me going to the airport and triggering the alarms. You can take satisfaction in the knowledge I will carry that with me until end of days.

I still think of you. I still remember the beautiful days we had together. Leaving Germany in the way that I did put a pit into my stomach. It has never gone. If you had trusted me, our life together would have been wonderful. We are joyous at the dawn and despondent at sunset. In your email you wrote that you were young and stupid; you said I made you crazy with the uncertainty, you lived in fear of me cheating. That is what drove you to lie. You wanted to make me jealous and feel what you felt. You said I should have held on longer that I wouldn't have regretted it. You betrayed me. What was I suppose to hold out for? An encore performance? You said you loved me in your last email and I never told you that I loved you. What is it that you loved? Did you love me because I spent money on you? Did you love me because sex clouded your mind? What does love mean to you? What is love? Does anyone really love anyone or do we only love ourselves? Perhaps you have answers; I don't...I only have the specter of death.

You are right, of course; I never did say I love you. I didn't need to say it. I proved it with my every action. Did I not accept full responsibility for everything by my silence? Wasn't I willing to die for you in *Sachsenhausen*? Action is truth; words lie. Marie, how I long to take you back into my arms and show you again my love. It is such a beautiful thought. But what would I find there, sorrow in your eyes and poison on your lips? I bounced between anger, dismay, longing and desire while I wrote this - not unlike the range of emotions you say you felt when we were together. Your decision to move on was the right one. A lifetime of resignation is superior to one minute of being with me.

I rose this morning coughing and could not fall back asleep. Why is it so hard for me to share how I feel? I keep trying to extract some meaning or purpose out of what passed between us. I feel there should be but I cannot find it logically. I can only feel it; the emptiness, the loss. Perhaps it was just a listless year where I hurt you because you hurt me. Perhaps there was no permanent commitment, the kind that works through any problem, the kind that forgives, rebuilds and loves. True love is the kind that puts the other above its own selfish desires.

This morning the rain came and washed away the beautiful snow. I wrote this poem for you, Marie. It is the fading voice of my life.

The swirling dream decays
The madness speaks slowly
Days pass between words
Then every word coincident
And every dream dead

Between the love I had
and the love I know is
Naked shame, sinewy and defined
The game and dance unlike hate
Are not proscribed

I make my last walk by slender trees
Who foresee what comes
But will not speak; they bend

their wills to push me away
When all I wanted was to remain
And be remains.

Your hand, held in mine
and the smile in your eyes are gone.
But not the image.
The memory of the feeling
is standing in the corner
in silent reflection.
Once formed by my kiss
Now strong in my undoing

I am where I started.

January, Saint Louis

Annelie, remember the words I spoke to you in the cafe? I told you I would take everything I had and throw it into the sea for you. I am sorry I said it. I know you well, Annelie, and those words showed weakness, the weakness you hate in a man. In your childlike mind, a man is an impenetrable fortress, flawless in its strength, overcomes all, never tires, and leads without error. It is clear I am not that man. If I can take any solace from this, it is simply that you, and you alone, heard my words, saw my weakness and rejected me. You are the only woman I have known who saw me as I would stand before God, full of doubt, weak and exhausted by life – most likely the last. Even if I survive this, I have closed the door.

Is it not surprising that I was exhausted? The time in prison had drained me of my strength but it was worse than even I realized at the time. I am dying from TB, a wonderful strain developed especially for me in the jails of South Africa by its incompetent populace who seem incapable of understanding what one needs to complete treatment. I cannot say in which holding facility I picked it up, since they moved me four times. I know that I spent the last of my time at Lindela Holding Facility in Krugersdorp. If I hadn't been transferred there by mercy of an officious policeman (who wondered why I was just sitting in jail without charges), I would most likely still be in jail.

I am sure it is not lost on you that this was the gift of your sister, who used her low level political influence to falsely imprison me. She met me just once at that Investment Society *braai* and decided I was bad for you. Why did she think I was seeing you? I didn't even want to return to school, but it was the only way I could stay for a year.

Did you know she sent an off-duty policeman to threaten me to stop seeing you? I told him there was nothing there and nothing to worry about. It's laughable because at the time we weren't romantically involved. That didn't happen until after my detention, did it? In fact, I was trying to just get on with my life and you chased me. Did you know they had me followed? I didn't. It was just thirty minutes after we met for the last time at the restaurant, where you showed up, "just by coincidence" that they picked me up walking home. The odd part is, I had gone there to meet a friend from Germany, Karl-Heinz, and he said to me, "I have a feeling a lot is about to change. There is something hanging over you like death."

If I had known that I was going to spend the next nine months in prison, I think I would have fought back and tried to make it to the consulate. Death would have been preferable. I say that as someone who is dying without any hint of hyperbole.

I am resigned to my fate but I am not bitter. I forgive your sister. Beautiful, fair Annelie, I wanted to take you from South Africa, from that growing pit of superstition, ignorance, corruption and incompetence it has become, but you would not go. The white knight arrives, but he is only welcome in the imagination of the fool. In the world we occupy, he is despised and spat upon. I knew this once but by some twist of fate, I forgot when I left prison. You, though young, taught me again. Chivalry, if it ever existed, is dead because there are no longer women who merit it. The West is fully occupied by narcissists and solipsists. I know because I am one of them.

I would not wish to be you and live frozen between the desires of two worlds... a child trapped in the expectations of her family and a young woman who wants to be free. You will not disappoint your family, so you only dream and take no action. I called your bluff when I offered to take you with me. When you said no, I knew there was no need for good-bye. There was nothing left to be said. You had already said it for both of us.

When I showed up at your apartment in Cape Town after they released me, I asked you to take me in until I had recovered and you did. That was a genuine act of love. I was essentially homeless. Everything in my apartment had been sold because the landlord thought I'd left the country. You took mercy on me and the tears in your eyes gave you away. Did you cry because my imprisonment was the price I paid for knowing you or did you cry because you saw my condition? I never wished to be pitied. I never considered myself as one who merits it. What I merit I am receiving, death. If I live, I will have to go 180 degrees from where I once was.

Something that was obvious to me in my year there you seem blind to. The Afrikaners will be forced out of Africa or buried. In two hundred years, the migration from Europe to Southern Africa will be nothing more than a piece of history. Their bones will be buried in the desert and their ancestors scattered throughout the Anglosphere. It's why I wanted to take you with me.

Do you remember when we first met? You intruded on a conversation I was having with Lauren. Lauren and I met at the UCT Big Bash and discovered we had the same class together in Afrikaans. Not long before that, I had broken up with my German girlfriend and I had no interest in seeing anyone. I went to school during the day (I was sick of school but the easiest way to get a visa) and at night I would go out to the clubs and drink. I was drunk a lot, something I had never done before. In some ways it was like being back in high school. Lauren liked the feeling that things could just blow up. Like me, she was a sexual refugee. There are no UN camps for us but we always find each other. We are the drifters on the planet hooking - up, hating life, and for a few minutes of pleasure, spitting a thousand fetching lies and melting into melancholy madness. Lauren and I knew each other and didn't have to talk about it. At that point I was pushing the self-destruct button with all the power I could. She was holding on to me and going for the ride. She knew there was no permanence, no peace and no chance for a future. She just wanted to enjoy the uncertainty, to go fast, to feel the rush and the thrill then go on her way. You came to push her down. Did you once say she was your friend? Women love to be loved more than they love each other.

That same night after I met you, you ingratiated yourself with Lauren and went out with us. I brought you along like a bratty sister, no fun and someone to look after. You are pretty to a fault. No one would question your intelligence but you are socially backward. You feel no obligation to keep a conversation going. You cut the threads with your silent tongue and your cold stare. It's not that you are shy. Unless it is about you or something you like, you are incapable of having a conversation. Even writing this now and remembering how I first got to know you, we hardly even spoke. Why were you interested in me? I ask because you never showed interest in a single thing I said. Marie, who left me, could charm every person in the room. You wanted everyone in the room to charm you.

That first night out turned ugly quickly. That one guy got upset that you wouldn't dance with him and grabbed your hand to try to drag you onto the dance floor. You looked at me with those eyes that said, "Do something."

I didn't have to because the bouncer was already on his way. When the guy saw him coming, he let you go. I knew better than to start a mess inside the club. The bouncers, the drug dealers, and the police all seemed to me to be playing on the same team. We left the club early, shortly after midnight. I wanted to lose you as soon as possible. Lauren read my irritation and she was a little afraid of me; I don't know why. I never raised so much as my voice to her. I treated her gently. She was a lot like me. Perhaps it was because she was afraid of what I might be capable of. What happened to her? After I came back from Lindela, she was gone and you didn't want to help me find her.

I thought that not rescuing you from that drunk would cause you to go away. It did not. You came around and tried to get between Lauren and me. You just showed up in the clubs we went to. You stopped to talk to me on campus. If I had been smarter, I would have suffocated you with praise and flattery and you would have gone. Instead, I took my feelings of dissatisfaction and aimed them at you. I would be sitting in my room, tossed and tortured by the thoughts I did not seem to be able to control, and instead of thinking of the one who cared for me, I would see your face. That's where it started - the aesthetics of you, that brought out a deep hunger for the unattainable. You were an archetype for an emptiness that cannot be filled in this world. At that time it never crossed my mind to desire anything more than to look at your soothing face.

You may wonder what finally led me to chase you. Prison had stripped me of all pretension. It tore down the defenses I had so carefully erected. To look upon you was a like a swirling opium dream, where the chatter of the restless mind goes quiet and you find yourself imagining that life is sweeter than it is. You see what you want and ignore the painful truth that all to soon you will return to the undistinguished life. We stand on this side of death's velvet curtain, the purple long gone, now brown and threadbare just one more inconsequential soul on a planet of a billion who want to feel loved. And so I fell for you, seeking the ideal and not what was there. But you showed me the cost of romantic yearning, the desire to rise above the mundane. You showed me there was no future with you. What fools men are, making our plans with the chimera.

How strange it must seem that I would write these words when all I ever did was kiss you hard, like I owned you. You slowly pushed me back, but not before you kissed me deeply, passionately. There were two short days of flirting and light touches. But pull away you did, because you had your own mirror of illusion and I showed no reflection, cast no shadow. Your heart told you the truth, your kiss confessed it but neither was so strong as your little girl fantasy of "the one." You tried to change the subject didn't you? You asked me where the scar across my left check bone came from. I stayed with you for three days and it took you that long to notice? You saw it on day one; you just weren't curious until it served your purposes.

I remember I told you how I sat in that godforsaken local jail for three months, the only white man in there, with a daily stream of male prisoners coming and going. The prisoners thought I was some drug dealer. One day I asked my jailer, "How much does such hatred cost, you know, to imprison someone on a bribe?"

He hit me in the face with his *sjambok*, just once, but it left a nice scar on my cheekbone. I like my scar because it is the cost of caring too much - and too little - for anything in this world. I never once thought I would fall into the trap of unrequited love but life can wear you down. Doubt can make you follow courses of action you wouldn't have considered previously. Failure can make you question all that you do and, in your weakness, to grasp for something to hold on to. A present memory of a pleasant past imagined as a perfect future. Men reach for women. Women reach for men. We reach for the union and the oneness. We grasp; we cling to each other desperate for eternity, but eternity is found only in death. We are made wanting to live forever and death is a consequence we do not escape. Consequences follow all our choices. Sometimes they fall on us but they often fall on others. Any one person may own their body but what they inflict upon it is borne also by those who love them.

Why did you take me in, flirt with me and withdraw? Annelie you are as inscrutable as any I have known. That afternoon sitting with you drinking tea on the day before I left, when I spoke those words, words I hoped would show you I was changed. High romanticism, but not what you wanted in a man. The more I ignored you and the worse I treated you the more you came around. It's sick what we do and do not do, what we want or think we want. Does being deliberately cruel make a man attractive? It's a broken world, filled with broken people in need of salvation. But when salvation came, we didn't want that either.

My nine months in detention and getting stabbed accidentally (when two prisoners were fighting) taught me that I really didn't want to die in Africa. But if you had asked me the week before I was picked up, you would have heard a different story. After I left Germany, there was a war raging in my head and it was spilling over into life. I was willing to fight anyone for any reason but as hard as I looked for trouble, I didn't find it the way I thought I would. It's strange how, when we want to fight, no one will and when we do not seek it, it comes with a kiss and a knife.

When I decided to leave Africa, I would have gladly taken you with me. I knew in my heart you would not go. I think you are happier clicking through those online dating forums, as if the right man is one picture, a click and two sentences away from realization.

You said you felt after I was detained that I was not the "one." There is no one that is the "one;" it is nothing more than a fairy tale of a young woman's heart. It's a fairy tale written again and again in the imagination. What exists is this moment, this person with you who is capable of loving you in a way most men cannot or will not. You treated me to a scrap of your life, a portion suitable for those we can dispense with quickly, hoping that there is no row. Of course, there wasn't one. I didn't wait to be told it was through, that it was pointless. I left Africa at once, regretting that I ever went there. Today, looking across the landscape of my limited time, I am not sorry I once knew you. I just wish it had been different.

You may wonder why I even bothered to write. What do I want? If this letter reaches you it is because I have died. I don't want anything more than to claw these words out of my mind, nothing more than putting words to the way I feel, to tell you unequivocally I wanted you and it was eating me alive. This is for you, Annelie, the truth of our short time together.

I stood at God's window
A blind view across creation
An invitation to jump
So I could feel the wind
On my pitiless descent.
But I was already dead to you
I could not separate this World
From the Next or separate the next
From the now, or the past from the present.
My mind was spinning
What was hungered for
Was not in this moment
Nor on this soil
Far away, as far as death is
In the mind of child or
Tears in the eyes of the executioner
Is home
You did not leave there
You may not return there
All you know is what you've lived
The rest are pretty stories
And one day they too
Will be forgotten like you
One man is interchangeable
With the next when seeking
The elusive one, the one

that tricks you every time, "The One"
Not this one, the one that
really loves you
He can go to hell.

RESIGNATION

January, Saint Louis

Shae, you received me as I was, scarred, devoid of innocence, dark, hardened to the world, full of contempt and for a short time, loved me. You are connected to the earth and pleasure; you are the perfect winter afternoon resting in streams of sun. You came into my life helped me believe, then you set fire to Eden. Or, perhaps, you were the desert wind that destroyed the mirage once and for all. If I have learned anything in my life it is that romantic love is a snare and a delusion. I can thank you for that. What the ancients knew I had to discover on my own. By living only for yourself, Shae, I have finally learned.

You are last American woman I will ever love. You hurt me deeply. Why did you cheat on me? I trusted you because things seemed so ideal. I suppose you had every right to pursue your personal happiness, to place it above a man you said you loved. I have a feeling, though, you won't find it. I have a feeling that you will look and look; you will say, "See it's just over here," or, "There, it is just around the corner." And when you get there, you will find nothing. I would not be surprised to find that you will dissipate yourself in the bed of many men and, seconds before you are no longer desirable latch onto some weak provider and try to have a family. Then the day will come when you will get bored and cheat. It doesn't have to be this way. You can choose another path - but that is where you are headed. Even the daughters of the Ozarks are living the post-modern fantasy. What part of me still cares enough to write you these final words? Perhaps it is the part that was blinded by passion, or the manic part that fell underneath your soothing touch.

After Africa I was the man who fell into an empty well and no one heard his call. It took me a summer to get my strength back. And now, my life is spilled water on a summer sidewalk and soon there will be no sign it was once here. I wish that, on the day you decided to move on, you had simply broken things off instead of cheating. Was it necessary to be test driven by my perfect replacement before you cast me into the outer darkness? Separating from you and facing death feel the same. The ancient pain returns.

From my earliest memory, I could taste the hint of death. Now the scent of it fills my nose and the taste permeates everything I eat. Death comes, in slow steps down the hallway and no one can see it coming but me. The hospital staff are happy and positive and blind; I see the sounds the footfalls of death makes, echoing in the hallway at 3:30 in the morning. But mostly I can smell it and taste it in my food.

I am wasting away from TB, as you well know. When I got sick, you got sick of me. As I was driving up to Saint Louis to consult with doctors, you were driven to move on. Good for you. Passion flatters, but it cannot grasp, it cannot hold. You once said that my intensity frightened you like waiting for a terrible storm - that my passion controlled me and I dominated you in bed. But my passion was not enough to keep you, was it? Passion just drains the life from the person who feels it. Passion rises and falls and extracts a cost on the fool who would carry it.

I am watching the snowfall outside my hospital window. It is just like the first snowfall on the property. Remember when you annoyed me and I picked you up and threw your naked body into the snow bank? I can still hear you squeal.

When I left Africa and bought my property along the Woods Fork Creek, I thought I had found a place to take my mind off of Africa. I went there to live like a hermit. I went there to forget the prior three years. I did what I always did when I moved to a new area- open a bank account and find a good attorney. I knew if I wired a large sum into the bank I would get to meet the president and he would be able to recommend a good attorney. John recommended your father. He was right. Your father has one of the finest legal minds I have ever known. He continues to look after my personal affairs, even now that I am in Saint Louis. I never told you but he told me not date you; he said you were fickle. He was wrong.

Shae, you are as crazy as I am. Remember that morning, lying in bed with your head on my chest? You said you would love me forever. I guess you still love me lying in the bed of another man. Who talks like that? What kind of person speaks of eternity so casually? It's rhetorical. Someone who has never thought about what it means, someone who lives one minute to the next and only for themselves, someone who understands pleasure but doesn't understand love. You are today who I was two years ago and just as mad. I heard in a song once: "To fall in love or out of love neither is ever real, you change the way you think; you change the way you feel."

Indeed, my facing death changed your thoughts. You thought about what it meant if I died, and decided you didn't want to stay around. And so, you cheated on me. It's hard to reconcile that act with the selfless, loving woman I once knew. I remember that time you showed up at the property early one Saturday morning while I was out hunting. I came in around 9:30 and I saw you standing out in the snow waving to me. I thought maybe something was wrong but as I got closer, I saw that wonderful smile and knew things were okay. You made me breakfast. Afterward, we went out in the snow and had a snowball fight. You might be short but you can throw. I should have known it was a set up, that four years of playing college softball you failed to mention.

Do you remember when we drove up to Springfield to go out to dinner last July? We were starting to make plans. We were starting to draw the edges of a future together. We had been together long enough that it seemed the natural course of action. I have to wonder how many times you have done this performance, building up the expectation, then detecting the edge of something better glittering on the horizon, destroying what was in your hand.

You used to trace the contours of the scars on my cheekbone and chest. Can you trace the contours of the ones in the mind? Is your commitment to personal satisfaction or to another human being? I know that for the better part of my life, I was not interested in anything permanent. Were we two souls one step out of time from each other? I don't really know.

I'm sick of feeling like I'm going crazy. No one knows it because I'm a fraud. I am out of my mind and no one can tell except you, the one who pretended to love me. No one can tell because I can function. I don't go to bed and sleep for two days. I don't stop taking care of myself. No one will see me out in the street talking to the empty air with a four-day beard. But I'm unwinding, a spool of endless thread peeling off the spindle and filling the room. I never reach the point where everything just falls down. I'm not cleaning the gutters at 3:00 AM. I'm not putting the pistol into my mouth.

God will not permit it. He would not let me die and he would not let me go over the edge. So I raced my motorcycle down Ozark highways as fast as I could, passing cars on the shoulder of the road past shocked drivers, shooting between cars in a lane of my own, daring God to kill me or cripple me. I have raced up and down the Springfield plateau looking for death and running from God. But God brings me down- not in some glorious act in celebration of human vanity, but through disease. I am crumbling a little each day. Today, even as I write these words, God is crushing me like a dried leaf between his hands, thoughtlessly, as his mind attends to more important matters.

I remember I warned you that you didn't want to ride with me, but you insisted. We took the ride to Wilson's Creek Battlefield fast enough to feel the cold breath of Civil War ghosts in our faces. When we stopped, you took off your helmet and jumped up and down in total exhilaration. I did not expect that. How could you be so excited when you had so little control? You trusted me and I trusted you. You arrived safely and I was sent to die alone.

When we took your horses to Busiek State Park and you gave me a crash course in riding, I had little control over the horse. You rode circles around me, teasing me. When I jumped off my horse to go after you, you took off and my horse followed yours leaving me stranded. I knew whose team that gelding was on. Does it make you smile to remember those days? How does one turn his back on someone he claims to love so easily? I still don't understand. I know you can't answer the question. All you could do is give me is a lengthy rationalization, which has nothing to do with the emotions that drove you.

In some ways, you never stopped thinking you were a tomboy trapped in a woman's beautiful body. Despite how you felt, you were one body and spirit, as feminine as any I knew. You had the softest hands that ever touched my face. A woman, a girl, eternal beyond the physical; fidelity with love was all I needed. I remember when you told me it was over, you tried to touch my face and I grabbed your wrist. You lost forever the right to touch me. There was no argument, no scene. You cried in some kind of self-pitying display and I left without saying a word. I did not answer your texts or emails. I cannot make you feel good about your decision. Everybody gets what they want.

Because of the illness, I needed to lock up the property and move back to Saint Louis. The fall rains came and I walked along the creek for the last time just after flood stage. I came to my favorite area, where I enjoyed catching small mouth bass with my fly rod. The heavy rains had destroyed the hole and the beauty was gone. And so I left, my mind no longer yearning for the beauty I was leaving behind. My home is the isolation room; my home is this bed.

For a time (before things got worse), I stayed with my brother Conor, whom you met. I can still remember the time Conor and Lettie came down with the kids and spent the weekend. We were kicking the soccer ball around and you stopped playing for a minute and said, "I want children one day." At the time, I thought in my vanity that you meant with me. I know now it was just an item on your checklist. You could have just as easily said, "One day I want a puppy," and it would have carried the same meaning. What was superficial for you was the anguish of another's heart. Later, when I was cooking for everyone, you came into the kitchen, held me from behind, and laid your head against my back. "Ryan, please don't make me cry, please don't hurt me, please don't let me down."

The first time we met I was cutting up the black oak that died from the lightning strike. You were sitting in your father's pick up while I signed some papers. When I looked up and into your eyes, you got out of the cab and joined your father, who introduced us. You saw something. You felt something. I did too. The attraction was immediate, strong and powerful. Your instincts were correct, but eventually they misled you. How happy are you today? Did you find what you wanted? Is he the kind of lover who can make you cry? I have discovered far too late that life is not worth living without someone to love, and love cannot last without commitment. I know you don't really like poetry because you say it's hard to understand. This is for you, nothing obscure just a remembrance of you and me and the black oak.

Beautiful Black Oak
Stretching up to the sky
Limbs arching over the land
How you could block the sun
On any summer day
For all your might, you had to stare
Upon the same monotonous ground.
120 years passed and only the contours of your scars
have changed.
The lightning was not your friend
It does not think of you
but does its duty
Stretching its arms across the horizon
While you stretched for the sky
It casts itself down from the heavens
While you were desperate to reach them
The lightning never tires
You could take no more
You dropped your leaves
and died.

My dearest Shae, I am ready. Good-bye.

LAMENT

I

You have seen me walking listless at strange hours
upset and changing like clouds tumbling across the sky.
You say my spirit is the charging animal,
bleeding from the hunter's mortal wound
before it stumbles, twisting its head in confused agony
and crashing into the dust of a desolate African plain.
But it is only a point in my life.
A specimen sliced for examination
and will pass as quickly as a breath
or a lover's sigh in the animal heart of the night.

I looked around
and this is a man's life.
Self-indulgent and unreflective,
An infinite sea of choices,
A monster of cruelty and despair,
A thoughtless creature plummeting,
into the darkness of physical pleasure
An aleatoric hunter with one cartridge,
Aiming for his dreams and shooting his future.

This is a man's life
A giant bridge of diamond light in a child's eyes
A rusting hulk leading to death.
An infinite causeway hung from the rotting moral fiber of man
And supported by the incomprehensible love of God.
It is object without form encompassing a timeless desert
There is no place to stand and see it all.
There are only narrow passages of clarity where you stood
The distorted visions of where you have been
And the hope of peace in the direction you are going,
But even the witless know there is no peace in the kingdom of men.

And you wonder at my behavior when you have never felt
A tireless penetration of pain or found yourself cast into
Dark days, tumbling, seeking a direction.
The countless times I lay in my bed, the liar and fraud
to the world,
Like a paralyzed man unsure of how to live,
Knowing only that death was the easiest path.

Have you woken in the night having dreamed the one you love is
dead?
This is how life has been.
The wretched fear that suddenly passes, the joy that turns to agony,
The constant unforgiving cycle of pain dissipating to happiness
Then faltering before fulfillment.
Each day that crawls
The next leans upon the minor changes
To blind the man to the pitiless rise and fall
Of laughter and tears.
We are finite as any decision
Eternal as any choice.
There is the endless desire to float through time
Like swans sleeping upon a lake
In the warmth of a new day's sun.
But the mind tires quickly of one thing
Like sprinters reaching the line.
And every man grows weary of life
Wishing to see the end of the bridge.

I crawled from my bed that became a marble slab
With perspiration crawling out like worms from dead flesh.
My mind was tumbling and screaming
Like a man falling from the building
I stood naked holding my face
And could not escape my own thoughts.
The image that is held most distant and pure
That has perfect edges
That brings absolute Joy
That has no comparable worth
Is the one that will never exist or take form
I saw a mirror in the distance but when I arrived it was shattered
And when I walked away and looked back I saw the mirror whole
again.
I heard a tone that touched a mood
But when I sought it out, it had never been sounded.
When I had stopped to listen, it came again.
I felt true love's gentle touch upon my sleeve
But when I turned to face her it was the wind moving the branch.
I walked through the woods to my home and when I arrived
I felt the touch again.

Never seen and known by all yet years of running only bring the
same thoughts
Re-lived in different metaphors.

And man wonders
Man wonders about man
Progress not man's distinctive mark
For there is none
Hypocrisy is man's distinctive mark and
The sweetest drink he will taste is his own self-pity.
He drinks in his madness
Trying to fill the emptiness of failure to be God,
Hardening himself to the suffering of life
Blinding himself to the suffering of others and
Driven by the mind that demands expression
Was not every emotion new at some point?
Today it tastes like metal in mouth,
Born into wonder dead in ennui.
And now
What can be said of these final moments?
This very empty moment
No different than all of life.

II

You romantic love
I wanted you never to leave me
Even today, decayed, stripped of pride
Hungry for death
I long to walk under your beautiful skies
To place my mind at ease in your perfect garden
There
The odd glimmers of different suns
Time slows
The cry of the heart fulfilled
Linger
Wash over me
End now the separation
Between man and woman
The brilliant blooms of blue flowers
Rise up to stare across the viridescent lawn
Its green subjects bending down in honor.

You romantic love
Intoxicated by your promises
I believed there was a still place
Where desire knows its limits.
Where the deepest fulfillment
Need only a single experience
Where passion deceives no one
Where we love by action
Without the vain desire to possess,
Or empty the joy from the other,
In the persistence of hatred's harmony,
In the voiceless cry of the heart.

Romantic love
Your intractable beauty
Has made me hungry for eternity
For on this side
In the realm of the prince of darkness
I will never taste the fullness of truth
Broken as I am
Broken by the knowledge of exhausting perfection.
No, romantic love as much as you promise
There is nothing to be found but
Passing emotion.
Time and eternity persistence of beauty
I can only see on a cross.
And still, I long for you late at night
Dying in my schemes of desire
Crawling desperately for the mirage.

III

Round and round turning out turning in
Splitting thoughts from feelings
Dividing life from living
Living from coins tossed into empty fountains
A smile, the pleasure, the shame
Born from the same hollow breaths
I know good and evil.
The one I cannot do or obtain at any price
The other I am.

For to know evil is to become evil
The depredation can only be seen
Staring into the mirror of perfection and
Starving for the permanence of things.
I have learned.
I am letting go in inches
And every inch measures my final steps
The deep pleasure of evil lasted for a season
Before it turned to despair
Lingering in the mind as long as life
But always leading to death
No man escapes the harvest of the Fall.
No man rejoices in his judgment.
Then slowly, softly descending like snow
Under moonlight
I find peace that brings the hatred of family
In the beginning was the Word
And Word came to man in mercy and love
So that nothing of value
Is lost.
And what is one man's life?

CHAPTER 8

They rode in silence the entire way to Mercy Hospital. Declan couldn't help but notice all the changes that had happened since he left. It was a little over eleven years. He had never come back after the funeral until now. Aidan came every other year with his wife at Christmas to stay with Conor so things still felt familiar. Declan did not break the silence, keeping his thoughts to himself. As they neared the hospital he started to think of his little brother. It had been strange for him to read the document, like he had opened a diary without permission, but as a physician it helped him understand Ryan's mental state. He knew the depression needed to be addressed if Ryan was going to live. Ryan needed something to tie him to this world, some level of hope - whether it was self-serving or selfless it mattered not.

Outside of small comments, they mostly walked in silence through the lobby. Inside the elevator, the weight of their youngest brother's illness weighed on all of them. For Aidan it was like going to see a distant relative; he really didn't know him. Conor felt he was visiting someone who put their mother through hell, and he could barely forgive him. And, Declan felt Ryan was a mixed-up kid who could have been his own son. He felt responsible for Ryan after their parents' death.

When they arrived at the nurse's station, they checked in. The hospital was no longer permitting unrestricted visiting. If they felt Ryan needed rest they would not permit visitors. And although Ryan had told Conor to come over, he was not aware of the restrictions. When they saw he was sleeping on the monitor, she told them they had to wait until he was awake.

A little over an hour passed and they were getting annoyed. The nurse finally came over and said, "He's awake. You can go in now."

Before they entered the room, they put on garments and surgical gloves, then washed their gloved hands in anti-bacterial foam. Finally, they put on N95 masks and entered the room. Ryan saw them come in and sat up in bed. He was the first to speak.

"I don't think we have all been together since the funeral. Am I right?"

"No, that sounds about right. How are you feeling?" Aidan asked.

"Pretty rough. I'm coughing a lot more and the night sweats are keeping me awake. I am changing two and three times at night. I can barely tolerate baby food."

This is not what Declan wanted to hear. The meeting with the other doctors needed to be pushed ahead. He would try to do that as soon as he left the room even if he had to go see everyone individually. He spoke up.

"I want you to know I have spoken with one the top experts in treating TB in the US and he said the medications you are on are the best choices we have now. He said it may take eighteen months but you will get better."

"I don't feel like I'm getting better."

"I'm going to meet with your doctors tomorrow."

"Declan, I want you know that without you I would have never finished school. I think without your help I would already be dead. I'm sorry I made your life hard for a couple of years. Conor, we never saw eye-to-eye and you were right - I did put Mom through hell and you were just trying to help. I'm sorry I was such a jerk to you. I hope you forgive me. Aidan, I never really got to know you because I was so eaten up with my own selfishness and problems I never took the time. I'm sorry. That's all I wanted to say."

"You're talking like you're about to die, Ryan. There's no need to apologize. I wasn't exactly around when you were growing up," Aidan replied.

They spoke over each other for a minute then it became quiet. A nurse walked in and gave everyone an excuse to look somewhere else.

"Hey Ryan, time for your meds."

As Declan was looking at the pills in their bar-coded containers, he noticed one that looked odd.

"I'm Dr. Altenburg, Ryan's brother. May I see your med list?"

"I'm not sure, Doctor, HIPAA privacy law and all. Not without the patience's permission."

"It's okay, Kara, I asked Dr. Isring to add my brother yesterday. Check the record."

Anthony pulled up his tablet and signed in. They stood patiently while he thumbed through the records. He looked up. "I found you. Would you be so kind as to show me a picture ID"

Declan patiently pulled out his driver's license and showed it to him. "Here's the list, Doctor."

Declan glanced at the five drugs listed on the sheet. Everything looked normal there. He picked up the one container and looked at the drug. It was methotrexate.

"Why is he being given an anti-inflammatory drug? This was not on the list Dr. Isring's nurse read to me. It's not on your list. He should be on oxyphenbutazone. I don't see it. What you have is methotrexate."

"I couldn't tell you why, Doctor, but ever since he's been in this room, I've been bringing him these five pills."

The look on Declan's face caused Aidan and Conor to look at each other to see if either one knew the significance. They both shrugged.

"Don't give that to him anymore." He said in a very commanding tone. "I need to talk to Dr. Isring."

Declan rushed out of the room with Aidan and Conor following him.

"Slow down Declan. What's going on?"

"Someone screwed up. That drug is used for rheumatoid arthritis and it suppresses the immune system. No wonder he's not showing any progress —excuse me, I need to talk to the head nurse."

He headed off to the nurses' station and although they couldn't hear what he said, the change on the nurse's face told them all they needed to know. They could see that Declan was livid. He pulled out his cell phone and made a call and then he walked back toward the room.

"I just spoke with Dr. Isring. He's in the hospital and he's on his way. This is a serious mistake. This shouldn't be happening. There are too many checks and balances. Someone needs to lose their job. Go back into the room and talk to Ryan. There's no need to upset him. I can handle things on this end."

As they were heading back into the room, a man exited the elevator and seeing the anger in his eyes, Declan knew it was Dr. Isring. He strolled up to him and extended his hand. They shook hands, and Dr. Isring spoke.

"Let's fix this first, then figure out how it happened."

"Nurse, please bring the correct dose of oxyphenbutazone and make sure it is in fact, oxyphenbutazone. Thanks."

The nurse left and went to the automatic dispensing cabinet. A few minutes later she returned. "Doctor, it's methotrexate. I would guess something happened at the manufacturer. It's not the first time."

"Okay, contact the pharmacy and see if they can help."

When Declan returned to the room, Ryan was dozing and Aidan and Conor were discussing a public court case. He interrupted. "I spoke with Dr. Isring. They've figured out the problem. It looks like it was a manufacturer packaging error. The impact cannot be known precisely, but it explains his at least partially the fact that he hasn't be responding to treatment."

Ryan opened his eyes. Though he was sleeping lightly, he heard every word. He said, "It's just as well. If that is my fate to not improve, so be it."

"Don't be fatalistic." Declan snapped. "You have to want to live."

"I'm tired. I'm not sure I do."

CHAPTER 9

Declan and Aidan were sitting in the guesthouse living room talking and half watching the financial news. "His blood work looked better this morning. I think he has a real chance, but I don't really think he wants to live. It's frustrating and annoying," Declan said.

Aidan replied, "Where does that come from? Dad wasn't like that. I'm not. You're not. Conor isn't."

"Mom told me that *Mamó* told her that *Daideo* had that temperament. He wanted to be a writer but he never finished anything. He was periodically depressed but never told anyone."

"He was not like that when we spent summers there."

"No, we never saw it but Mom did when she was an adult. She didn't notice it as a child."

"It really makes you wonder what is it that allows some to deal with stress and others to fold under it."

"Almost every talent and skill is a double edged sword. A person brilliant in one area will have a learning disability in another. Creative people will fight with depression, mania or both. He refused to talk to a psychologist, you know. The only person with any counseling training he will see is that Lutheran pastor. Didn't you see Grandpa's Book of Concord in German on his desk?"

"No, I didn't. It's hard to believe he's swallowed the fairy tale hook line and sinker. We certainly weren't raised that way."

"The pull to superstition is strong. It defies reason. We aren't all that far from the cave. When you were on the phone this morning with a client, Conor brought it up when he saw the Book of Concord. He recognized it from Grandpa's house. I didn't. You know Conor, he would pick an argument with a drowning man."

"Heh, yeah, that's him. He loves to argue."

"He said to Ryan, 'I see you have *Opa's* book of fairy tales.' Ryan didn't take the bait. He just replied, 'How did you arrive at that conclusion?' He made Conor defend himself. I just cut it off right there by changing the subject but Ryan said, 'You can change the subject but you can't change the eventuality. Both of you will die and face God one day. What is the point to your lives? You live like you are immortals. Perhaps as some level you believe that.' Conor started to open his big yap but I bumped his foot and he let it go."

Aidan smiled. "Conor is so thick. He wants to argue religion with a chronically ill person. I don't blame Ryan for grabbing the nearest crutch. He needs something to believe in."

"Exactly. Aidan, did you read the letters from Ryan to those women?"

"I sort of scanned them a couple of times."

"Well, there are two women in those letters who seemed most important to him, Marie and Isabel. Conor said he remembered Isabel vaguely. I asked him if the private detective had found contact information. He expects a report this afternoon. If he has the information for those two, then I am going to see if they will call, write or visit him. Anything at all to boost his spirits —if he can reconnect — then there is a real chance he will want to live. It's a gamble but I don't know what else to try."

"I think that is all we have. We can visit him regularly and try to boost his spirits. The trouble is, I have to fly back on Saturday. I have to be in court Monday morning for an arraignment."

"I hear you. I have to leave Friday."

They couldn't escape a feeling of guilt at leaving with Ryan's health so uncertain. The days of sending a messenger to a field to tell of a death in the family were long past. To stand at the bedside when the one you love dies is simply luck.

Conor knocked on the door and entered. He was holding an envelope. "This is what I got back from Ted," he said handing the envelope to Declan. "It looks like he found everyone except the girl in the first letter. There wasn't enough information to do anything with that."

Declan replied, "I think the only two worth contacting are Marie and Isabel."

"I guess." Conor replied.

Declan opened the envelope and looked at the list. His eye went to Marie's name. She was living in Austria, where Ryan had last seen her. He had a phone number and an email address, with the word "verified" next to each. Next he looked at Isabel's name and saw a business address with a phone number in San Francisco. She was two hours behind Central time, so he would start there. He got up, took out his cell phone, and walked out of the house and into the courtyard.

CHAPTER 10

"Good Afternoon, Córdoba Floral Design," a soft, pleasant, voice answered.

"Isabel?"

"Speaking."

"Hi, this Declan Altenburg. We actually never met. I believe you know my younger brother, Ryan."

There was a momentary silence then she answered, "That's a name I haven't heard for a long time. How is he?"

"That's the reason that I am calling. He contracted tuberculosis in Africa and he is dying. He is being treated and should recover but he is not. The thing is I don't believe he wants to live."

"I'm sorry to hear that."

"I want to ask a favor. My brother wrote a letter to you that he asked only be sent if he dies. It is a remembrance of your short time together. Well —I think that if you could visit him, email or call it would help. Pick up his spirits."

"I see. I'm not sure it would make any difference. We were just kids the last time we saw each other. Visiting is out of the question; I have to do flowers for weddings every weekend this month. If you give me his email address, I guess I can send him a note."

"Sure, it's easy to remember: ryan@altenburg.us. If you give me your email then I will send you the letter. Just read it first then email him. I think the context will help."

"My email is isa@cordobafloral.com. "

"Thanks, I will send it right away. I appreciate you trying to help. Bye for now."

"Good-bye." She hung up her phone. *That was really strange. Ryan, out of the blue —odd that he never wrote me and now he is dying.*

§

The phone rang again while she was thinking about Ryan. *Stupid phone never stops ringing. How am I going to get everything done for the wedding? It's probably that crazy groom's mother who won't stop meddling.*

"Good Afternoon, Córdoba Floral Design."

"Hello Mija!"

"Hola Papi."

"Are you coming by for dinner still?"

"Yes, if I can ever get out of here on time. I am behind on the table centerpiece for the wedding this weekend."

"Well, don't rush. We can hold dinner an hour if you want."

"That would be perfect. . . Papa, do you remember that boy I was friends with when we lived in St. Louis? I found out he is dying from TB. His brother called me."

"Of course, I remember him. You two were very close. It was unhealthy. After we moved here, I had to put a stop to it. I deleted his emails and your mother threw away some letters. I'm sorry he is ill. "

"You did what?" She was incredulous. "Did I hear you correctly? You deleted his emails and threw away his letters?"

"It was for you own good. You had talent in ballet and you wouldn't have been able to turn professional pining for that boy."

"I'm stunned. I can't believe you did that."

"At thirteen we are not qualified to judge what's best. It was a long time ago. I don't know if I would do the same today."

"Do you realize how badly hurt I was?"

"Yes, but you focused on dancing and it turned out well."

"Turned out well? I burned out and quit my third year in the company."

"Yes, but you got a design degree and look how well you are doing now."

"I'm sorry; I can't even talk to you now." And with those words she hung up. She went into the back room her mind racing through the past. She looked at the centerpiece and no longer felt like working on it.

Sitting down at her desk she started checking her emails out of habit. She saw one from Declan Altenburg and clicked on it. There was an attachment and she double clicked it, not even bothering to read the body of the message.

§

Declan had finished composing the email and clicked *Send*. He typed the URL into his browser from the sheet Conor gave him which linked to the faculty page at the *Universität Wien*. Marie's picture came up along with a description. *It's been too long since I read German,* he thought. He remembered the awful German lessons his Grandfather paid for when he was little. *What does she do?* He looked up and saw a link for English and switched the language. She was a research assistant in the biology department.

He wasn't exaggerating in his letter. She's beautiful. I hope her English is better than my German.

He checked his watch. It was 6:00. Austria was seven hours ahead. He didn't expect to hear back until sometime tomorrow. He was hungry. He would go see if his brothers wanted to get a steak.

"Well, I sent the email to Marie with his contact information. I will see if she responds." Declan said. "I'm hungry. You want to get a steak?"

"You bet," Aidan responded.

"Conor?"

"Sounds good to me."

"Where do you want to go?"

"Is there a Fleming's or Ruth's Chris?"

"Both."

"Which is closer?"

"Fleming's."

"Okay, let's go there. Let's see if we can get a table first."

"Let me call, since I have taken a number of clients there. I'm going to ask Lettie if she wants to go to dinner." Conor said and then exited the guesthouse.

While they were waiting for him to come back, Declan's phone buzzed from an email. He looked at the screen. It was from Marie.

Dear Declan:

I am deeply sorry to hear about Ryan. Although I haven't read the letter yet, I will. Unfortunately I cannot leave my job at this time to visit him but I will call him and email soon.

With kind regards
Marie

What more could he ask? A lot of pretension drops when we know someone is facing death. He would have to tell Ryan tomorrow that he sent the letters. He wasn't sure how he was going to react.

CHAPTER 11

Ryan was still bedridden. Was he worse? Was he better? He couldn't tell; the pain was roughly the same and he had good days and bad days. His brothers were gone, returning to their families and homes. Now that Conor and Lettie had what they wanted, they had not stopped by. Emily had texted him that morning. *"I want to come visit u mom says no too busy."*

Last week was disruptive for everyone and they have to catch-up. I'm glad they came by. Although he was unhappy with Declan's decision to send the letters, he was too tired to fight with him. He was physically at the point where it didn't matter who saw him dressed or undressed. He just didn't care. There was no dignity left. He had no goals except one. One that he would not admit to anyone, he wanted to live.

He was thinking to himself, *In the daily lives of people, they rarely consider their own death even when grieving the death of those they love. Man is born with a blind spot to his own mortality. God created man to live forever but death came from sin. Death is not natural. Those that face death and welcome it, rarely feel connected to those around them. When you feel close to your friends and family, you are not ready to leave. When illness, sorrow and age wear you down, you are ready because of exhaustion not because death has any appeal. Who wants to face God?*

His thoughts were interrupted by the sound of a loud voice, "Holy crap, this place is like a science fiction movie. I'm glad I didn't bring a pony keg."

He looked up and saw three of his fraternity brothers walk into the room. It had been almost seven years since he saw them last.

"Don't you losers have jobs?"

"Hey, it's Presidents' Day. We're honoring the office by visiting the sick, the infirm, the forgotten. People like you, Altenburg. You look great." he said sardonically.

"I wish I could say the same for you guys. I see you haven't put a fork down in the last seven years, Roach."

They all laughed and Ryan began a coughing jag which dragged on long enough that his friends started to look concerned.

"Seriously brother, how are you doing? You should have let us know," said John Murphy, the one they called Roach. He was given the name during hell week for his ability to eat or drink anything without throwing up.

"I'm extant. I didn't have anyone's contact information. How did you find me?"

"Your brother Conor. He was representing a husband in a divorce case and I'm representing the wife. I saw his name and asked if you were related. He told me where you were."

"I'm glad you guys came by, really."

"Well, don't go all soft on us Altenburg," Bernie Levine said. Bernie was the only Jewish member of his fraternity during his four years in school. He took a lot of teasing because of it. It used to make Ryan angry and he didn't think it was funny. If it bothered Bernie, he never showed it. Bernie had been his big brother when he was a pledge.

Ryan laughed at his remark. It's the same thing he told him during hell week when he thought about quitting. "I'm not quitting, big bro."

"Good, because your behind on your alumni dues." Bernie's joke broke the tension and everyone laughed.

Steve Hailer spoke next, "Ryan, we were talking on the way over here about that time when you were a pledge and suplexed that guy in front of the frat house after he grabbed your girlfriend's butt."

"Heh, I remember. She wasn't my girlfriend exactly. We sort of hooked up. In any case, he brought it on himself. He was smiling when he did it. He wasn't smiling when his friends helped him to the car. I ran into him on campus the next day and he apologized. He was an okay guy. He just got drunk and it impaired his impulse control. I fine tuned it for him."

Roach said, "The time I remember was when you pushed that redneck out of the house who was stupid drunk and he came back with his two friends. You walked out of the house to talk to them and they started swinging. You beat the shit out of all of them."

"Oh yeah," Steve said, "that first guy, you just kicked his front leg out from under him and he was finished. You knocked the other two down with punches. Bernie pulled you back when you tried to kick them in the head."

"I kept him from going to jail." Bernie didn't join in enthusiastically because he never liked Ryan's flash temper and propensity to violence. He was always telling him to calm down. When Ryan was a freshman, it didn't take much provocation to set him off. Over the next three years he learned to control himself, but Bernie graduated before it happened. It was Bernie and his father that got Ryan interested in trading. He spent a week at Bernie's home in Mission Hills Kansas over spring break of his sophomore year and Bernie's father taught Ryan a working trading approach. After a lot of initial success with it, he eventually modified it from a futures trading system to one he could use in the currency markets.

Ryan asked, "What are you doing these days Bern? Trading like your father?"

"No, investment banking. I like helping mid-tier companies grow."

"Really? Well if I survive this, we should talk. I learned a lot from your dad. I still use his basic system."

"Sure, no problem. Do you want to get into the field?"

"No, I want to buy a company eventually. Something in manufacturing."

"Sure, we'll talk when you're on your feet."

Ryan turned to Steve. "I know Roach is a shyster like my brother but what are you doing to stay out of jail?"

"I started out writing software for HP but I didn't like it, so I switched to the sales side."

Roach jumped in. "He didn't like writing boring crap no one can understand so instead he sells it."

While they were laughing a young woman with long, wild, curls walked in. Without a word she slipped on the mask and washed her hands. For a brief moment, her slow graceful movements and athletic body transfixed them. Bernie looked back at Ryan and saw a change in his face. It was a look he had never seen before. "Guys, let's step out and give Ryan some air."

Roach answered, "What? Oh, sure."

They walked out, smiling as the young woman passed them, Roach winked at Ryan and bit the heel of his hand smiling. That is not how Ryan felt. He sat up slowly and felt some trepidation.

"Hi Ryan. I don't know if you recognize me. It's me Isabel."

"I know, Isa. I would recognize you if it had been fifty years."

"I spoke to your brother Declan."

"He told me."

"I have so much to say. . . . I'm sorry for the loss of your mom and dad."

"Thank you."

"I want you to know that I never received your letters or emails. My parents prevented it. They knew about us. They thought it was best if we never saw each other again. It hurt me deeply because I thought you turned your back on me."

Ryan did not reply but continued to look at her.

"Declan does not believe you want to live. That is not the boy I once knew. I was going to send you an email but then I read your letter —it touched me deeply."

She reached out her hand, placed it in his and said, "You wrote that separation is indistinguishable from death. If that is true, then this moment is life."

He coughed briefly behind the mask and then looked at her. She could see the smile around his eyes.

ABOUT THE AUTHOR

Quoddam in an author living in St. Louis, Missouri. When he was child he used to tell his family he wanted to be a writer or a scientist. He was neither until now.